ABOUT THE AUTHOR

James Warden was a teacher for forty years and retired in 2006. He now enjoys his retirement as much as he enjoyed his time in the education service and is catching up on those things which he left undone and ought to have done – in particular, his writing. He writes every morning between nine o'clock and noon, for thirty-six weeks of the year.

He is fortunate enough to be able to act in several Norwich theatres – the Maddermarket, the Sewell Barn and, with the Great Hall Players, at the Assembly House – and this experience informs his writing. His stage adaptation of Laurie Lee's *As I Walked Out One Midsummer Morning* was performed at the Sewell Barn Theatre in November 2009. His original play, *Letters from a Boy in the Trenches*, which was based on the letters of a WW1 soldier, was performed in Marchington, Staffordshire in 2015.

James is married – for the second time – and lives in Norfolk. He and his wife travel as much as possible. They have visited Italy (where they were married in 2002) several times, Canada, Bermuda, Egypt, India, the Czech Republic, New England, Poland, Slovenia, Antarctica, the Falkland Islands, Alaska, the Galapagos Islands, and Australia. In 2018, they travelled across the USA on Route 66. They have also taken several holidays in various Mediterranean resorts – the basis for his first novel, *Three Women of a Certain Age*, which was published in July 2010.

During his years in education, he wrote about twenty play scripts for children. These included the one that formed the basis for his children's story, *The Great Gobbler and his Home Baking Factory at the North Pole*, which he wrote in 1982 and published in December 2010.

He has three sons by his first marriage, and they inspired two of his novels – *The Vampire's Homecoming*, which was published in 2011, and *The One-eyed Dwarf*, published in 2012. With them and his first wife, he also travelled to the southern states of North America, France, Germany (West and East), Estonia and what was Czechoslovakia.

WRITING BY JAMES WARDEN

Stories of Our Time
Three Women of a Certain Age (2010)
The Age of Wisdom (2015))
Swinging in the Sixties (2016)
Benjamin Rudge: a Tale of the London Riots of '11
(2024)

'Tales of Mystery and Imagination'
The Vampire's Homecoming (2011)
The First Rendlesham Incident (2017)
The Search for Edwin Drood (2020)
The Haunting of Thornham Staithe (2022)
The Lawyer of Skagway
(To be published in 2026)

Stories for Children
The Great Gobbler and his Home-Baking Factory at
the North Pole (2010)
The One-eyed Dwarf (2012)

Biography
The Boy in the Photograph: Bill Pieri's autobiography
(2014)
A Child of the Fifties: autobiography of my childhood
(2017)

BINGHAM AND THE LOST YEARS

BY

JAMES WARDEN

Grosvenor House
Publishing Limited

This book is published by
Grosvenor House Publishing Ltd
Link House
140 The Broadway, Tolworth, Surrey, KT6 7HT.
www.grosvenorhousepublishing.co.uk

This book is a work of fiction. Any resemblance to
people or events, past or present, is purely coincidental.

A CIP record for this book
is available from the British Library

ISBN 978-1-83615-209-5

Chapter One
NO PRECISE PIECE OF EVIDENCE

Bingham had spent the best part of the morning trying to coax the innards from a Turk's Turban, but the pumpkin resisted his attempts at securing enough flesh to turn into the soup Lina intended to make for their lunch.

Normally, this would not have been his responsibility: on the first day of their married life, Lina had banned him not only from the kitchen but also from the house. She considered the home to be her domain. "You bring back the rabbit, Bing, and leave the cooking to me," she'd said. He took her point, although her chosen phrase was probably not the most suitable, since they were both vegetarians.

Having spent his adult life to forty, his age when they met, more-or-less looking after himself, Bingham, at first, found this new-found arrangement strange, but the arrival of four children in rapid succession gave him plenty to do, aside from looking after the home.

On that morning, Lina was called away: one of the old ladies in the village had suffered a fall, her son phoned Lina and so Bingham was left with the pumpkin.

He wasn't a moody man – his worst enemy would have acknowledged Bingham's mellow temperament – but the resistant pumpkin had aligned itself with another quandary, one imposed by his youngest son, Ben, a chemist who worked at John Innes in Norwich. Ben was due to arrive sometime that morning, ready to take his father on what he euphemistically described as "a walking break". Only the walking wasn't his son's real reason for driving the two of them to Upton-on-Churnet, and Bingham had reservations about Ben's intentions.

It was autumn, after all, Bingham's favourite season. It had been so his whole working life; settling into the routine of teaching and learning in September had always given him a focus, a purpose and a relaxation. His generation of teachers always looked upon that term as the one where the school was settled for the year and where most learning took place; if the children weren't keen and receptive then, they never would be; it was in the autumn – free from the colds and sniffles of winter and the distractions of summer – when imaginations were fired and futures forged.

Besides, the season had its own attractions and beauties; the harvest had been reaped and golden cylinders adorned the stubble; in the hedgerows, sprays of berries hung heavy with fruit, and birds were fattening themselves ready for the cold; swallows gathered for their flight south; the harvest moon rose early in the evening and he and Lina would walk from their farmhouse home along the country lanes that led down to the village of Northfield, watched by *their* barn owl sitting on a fencepost; early in September the horse chestnut leaves turned yellow and then red and, finally, russet, and the other trees followed suit, each in their own time until the lanes and byways were strewn with falling gold; smoke filled the air, the fresh smoke of burning wood and leaves; mushrooms, toadstools and the delicate, mauve blossoms of the autumn crocus pushed up through the moist soil or from fallen branches; sometimes, ducks from the north would arrive to winter on their pond, the pond Lina had made her own; his favourite wild animal, the squirrel, might be seen scrabbling for cobnuts if Bingham was lucky.

Why on Earth would he want to travel to Staffordshire to listen to the story of a man who claimed to have been wrongfully imprisoned for fourteen years?

In the summer, Bingham had stayed with his son in Norwich during the time he was acting in a play at the Maddermarket Theatre. It was the first play Bingham had taken part in for three years, his encroaching deafness making acting difficult. But it had been a good experience; the young people in the cast had been considerate and helpful, nudging him on if he missed a cue and giving him the thumbs-up when he was ready in time. Their diction, too, had been excellent: what he failed to hear, Bingham was able to read on their lips. Agatha Christie's own adaption of her novel, *Towards Zero,* had received its premiere that summer and Bingham was proud to have been part of the production.

His son had an apartment on Westwick Street, only a short step from the theatre and it was during one of their conversations following his rehearsals that the case of Raymond Dowdall was mentioned.

Ben learned of the young man's "plight" – as he put it – from a university friend who came from the same market town. The story went (and Bingham's reservation hung on the fact that it was only a story and probably mere gossip) that the young man – he was 17 at the

3

time – had been convicted of a murder, despite there being no precise piece of evidence against him, through a botched police investigation that smelled of slackness, if not corruption.

Bingham had no time for the public's fascination with the idea of police corruption: he'd known too many good coppers for such a view to hold much credibility with him, and it was this impression that explained his reluctance to undertake the "walking break", a break he was aware his son thought might give him a chance to "sniff around".

The bare bones of the story (as told by his son who Bingham could see was only repeating what he had learned from his university friend) was that a young woman had been found murdered below the wall of a churchyard at Upton-on-Churnet. Raymond Dowdall worked at an estate agents in the town and was in the habit of eating his lunch in the same churchyard every day. He was described as a quiet lad, content in his own company, and enjoyed the view from the church across the valley of the Churnet. The churchyard was surrounded by a stone wall on the far side of which there was a drop of several hundred feet to a footpath that followed the river. It was here the woman's body was found beside a dense copse of beech trees. Raymond Dowdall had seen the body as he leaned over the wall and immediately ran back to his place of work where he asked his employer, Mr Roberts, to phone the police. Mr Roberts took the boy back to where he claimed to have seen the body; this involved a walk by another route because the footpath was not accessible from the churchyard. Once he was sure the boy's story was true, Mr Roberts phoned the police. In what seemed no time at all, the police had combed the area for evidence and arrested Raymond Dowdall on the strength of their finds. He was formally charged within forty-eight hours. This had occurred in the autumn of 2004 and in February the following year, the young man had been tried, found guilty and detained at the "Queen's Pleasure", a phrase that seemed to amuse even those who believed in Raymond Dowdall's innocence.

It was, perhaps, this sense of the ridiculous that had cautioned Bingham against reading too much into what his son had to say on that summer evening as they sat comfortably sipping a glass or two of whisky in the Westwick Street apartment.

Bingham was only too aware that people – even men, at times, he would acknowledge to Lina – enjoy gossip. He listened while his son related the story, which he probably picked up between 2006 and 2009 when he graduated; by that time, Raymond Dowdall would have been in prison for up to four years, and the story was, no doubt, still fresh in the minds of the people in the small market town. His thoughts ran to the parents and he wondered – he knew – how he would feel if the boot was on his foot.

He admired his son, a feeling that ran to all four of his children although he was aware that he had always felt particularly close to Ben. The boy had done well for himself: a first at the UEA and holiday work with John Innes that eventually led to an offer of full-time employment. He was a grafter and had risen in the esteem of the firm during his ten years with them. He had Lina's dark, Italian looks: the thick, wavy hair and what appeared to be a permanent tan. He was lean like

Bingham, but taller, lounging easily at just over six foot on the Chesterfield sofa.

The apartment – a studio, really – had been furnished from second-hand emporiums with the help of one of his sisters, Cecilia, who knew a thing or two about vintage furniture. Concealed lighting and table lamps gave the place a welcoming warmth and Bingham – an obsessively tidy man – admired the fact that nothing was out of place. In one corner of the studio stood a baby grand and beside this an alto saxophone that Ben played in a local jazz group.

The fact that the boy seemed happy in his own company and that of a few friends might have troubled some parents but neither Bingham nor Lina was perturbed since they'd both been of a similar disposition until they met at the London Coliseum in 1984.

The memory of that evening was running through his head as he struggled with the pumpkin, waited for his son to arrive and Lina to return.

His wife was the first to appear, relieved that she'd comforted the elderly villager and called in the vicar to sit with her while she recovered. Clemency Freeman was a hands-on clergywoman, much admired by Bingham, an atheist of the old-fashioned kind, and Lina, a Roman Catholic by upbringing but an active member of the local Anglian church, St Mary Magdalene.

"I'll have the pumpkins displayed before you get back, Bing – unless you want me to wait?"

"No, no, Lina, you go ahead."

"You don't sound convinced."

"I'm not."

"The break will do you good and you like Ben's company. You don't see enough of each other as it is."

"No," he replied, an answer that Lina knew often covered a wide range of feelings and, at that moment, indicated he'd rather be at home with her arranging the pumpkins.

The idea had come to them eight years before when they'd visited New England, where they'd both felt immediately at home. In Stowe, they found pumpkins placed along the tops of walls, edging the pavements around their hotel and arranged with flowers in doorways. Once back home, they'd taken the idea aboard and each year created a pathway from their front porch to the little gate that led down from the Italianate garden fronting the house and placed more pumpkins along the top of the wall that protected Lina's pride and joy from the north winds, which occasionally cut across the old farmyard she'd inherited from her parents.

She walked over to Bingham, put her arms round his shoulders, hugged him and leaned in close to his chest.

"Are you tired?"

"Yes – at seventy-five, I suppose I must expect it."

"They needn't be long walks. Ben will understand – but it isn't the walking, is it?"

"No."

"You don't think there's much to Ben's story, do you?"

"No."

"You're a listener, Bing, and there aren't many of those around. Go with Ben and just listen. You're sensitive to people, and he knows you'll pick up on things he might miss."

"You can't butter me up, Lina."

"Yes, I can ... Ben first told me about Raymond Dowdall when he came home from university one Christmas. Ben was great friends with the boy who told him the story – Mervyn, wasn't it? – and there's no doubt Mervyn was upset. He and Raymond were at school together, and he believes him to be innocent. If you find there's nothing to the story, you're no worse off. You'll have had a nice walking break with your son and it will put Ben's mind at rest that he's done what he can."

"Do you know what brought this up so recently? Ben left university ten years ago."

"They're still in touch – that's social media for you. We had to write letters, which we never got around to doing; all Ben's generation need to do is click a mouse. I think it's a good thing."

"I won't argue with that," replied Bingham, returning his wife's kiss and feeling better for her little homily.

"I think there's enough pumpkin flesh here, Bing. I'll get on with that soup. Ben said he'd be here by midday."

Bingham made them both a coffee and sat admiring Lina as she boiled the pumpkin with onion, garlic and a vegetable broth before blending the mixture smooth and adding a dash or two of herbs and pepper. Looking down, he saw their four dogs watching with him. From the oven rose the smell of warm bread, and he knew, not for the first time that morning, why he really did not want to travel north to Upton-on-Churnet.

"You've done what?"

"I've arranged for us to visit Raymond on the way," replied Ben, "You can't just walk in and say 'hello', Dad. Prisons aren't residential care homes."

"Possibility not," replied Bingham, thinking that one or two care homes he'd come across seemed to resemble prisons, in as much as the residents seemed unable to leave (some having been pursued if they tried), were confined to one room for most of the day's twenty-four hours and experienced restricted visiting times.

"Visiting hours are restricted, you see, Dad, and so I had to arrange with Raymond's parents that we'd be the ones visiting today. They didn't mind. In fact, they were pleased that you're taking an interest."

"You've been what's called 'pro-active', Ben. Which prison are we visiting?"

"Her Majesty's Prison Dovegate. It's near Uttoxeter. The authorities always try to keep prisoners as close to their families as they can."

"And Raymond's parents still live in Upton?"

"Yes. Dovegate is their nearest category B prison."

"Category B?"

"It's for those prisoners who may pose a risk to the public but who don't require maximum security because they're unlikely to try to escape."

"So, your friend still poses a risk, does he?"

"No, but he's never admitted his guilt and so they won't downgrade him to a category C prison," replied Ben, watching his father's face as much as the road ahead. "He's done well in Dovegate. They have an adult training programme and Raymond has studied for a degree."

"In?"

"Architecture. He's interested in old buildings."

Where else could you study for a degree without incurring unreasonable debts? It was a sudden thought and Bingham didn't like it or himself for thinking it. As a man who enjoyed walking his dogs each day, he could well imagine what kind of hell it would be to suffer incarceration. He looked at Mollie, the Old English Sheepdog mongrel who he'd befriended on his last case, relieving her of the woman owner who had no time for the animal. Since then, Mollie had become distressed if ever Bingham was away for long and so Lina suggested she might enjoy the walking break. He fondled her ears and turned to his son.

"What was the relationship between your university friend, Mervyn, and this young man?"

"They were just friends. They were at school together. Why do you ask?"

"No reason. I was just trying to form a picture of the people involved. Will Mervyn be there – in Upton, I mean – when we arrive?"

"I don't know. He works in Stoke and lives there, as far as I know. We might meet up. That'd be good. I've booked us into The White Hart. It's a nice little pub in the town. It's run by the community."

Bingham had expected problems when they arrived at H M Prison Dovegate, but the opposite proved to be the case: the officers on duty could not have been more obliging. He and Ben reported to the visitors block and were surprised to find it empty.

"You're late, sir, but never mind. We'll get you through as soon as we can. The other visitors went in fifteen minutes ago. Raymond's parents suggested you might like a private room. If you'd just step this way, gentlemen, we can commence the search."

'Step this way' proved to be a tidy step along several corridors, each secured by a gate or door that had to be opened and then locked. Eventually the officer led them into a small office, its walls festooned with notices of regulations, where he turned and enquired, with noticeable embarrassment, whether they objected to a strip search.

"It's regulations, gentleman. You'd be surprised what visitors smuggle in – and how!"

The suggestion didn't bother Bingham, who had a rough sense of humour, but Ben disliked stripping in front of anybody. Some years before when Bingham and his two sons had taken a mud bath in Parnu, a small town in Estonia, it was his youngest son who had been first to grab at a towel. Bingham grinned at his son, a grin that said: 'This was your idea'.

"If you'd put your clothes on the chair, gentlemen. Shoes, keys, watches and coins in the tray. Down to your undies and socks, please. Arms raised! There we go. All done."

'All done' involved the warder running his arms up and down their legs, arms and sides, while another officer examined the items in the tray and the pockets of their coats. Catching Bingham's eye, the second officer grinned.

"Drugs, sir. We have to look."

"I've never taken drugs, nor supplied them, in my life," replied Bingham

"I can tell that, sir. I knew the moment you walked in."

"How?" asked Bingham, seeing that the man wanted to be asked.

"The colour of your skin – it's not pallid like that of a druggie – your nose isn't disappearing, your lips aren't cracked, your arms were clear when you stripped, your teeth aren't rotten, your eyes aren't shifty."

"But you searched my pockets, anyway? Did you expect to find something in my notebook?"

"You'd be surprised how much heroin can be concealed in the spine of a notebook, sir. Reading is a preferred occupation of many of our customers – even those who can't read," replied the officer, with a knowing grin, waiting for Bingham to enquire further.

When he didn't, the man carried on.

"Ever read *Ulysses*, sir?"

"Yes."

"Tidy read, isn't it, sir? And a book with a large spine! You'd be surprised how many of our customers enjoy a big read, sir. John Grisham is a great favourite, closely followed by Dan Brown and the classics – preferably in hardback, of course. Paperbacks have never really taken on in Her Majesty's prisons. Embossed covers are a reading must, too, sir. Underneath, they can hold as much heroin as the flap of a brown envelope or a postage stamp ..."

"That's enough, Jack," cut in the first officer, "You'll be giving Mr Bingham ideas. You'll excuse our sense of humour, sir."

"I'm sure it helps," replied Bingham.

"It's essential, sir. Without it, you'd go nuts in here. When we reach the interview room, sir, always remember, hands on the table and nothing to be exchanged between you and the prisoner. You do understand?"

"Yes, we understand," replied Ben, irritated by the officers' bonhomie as much as his father was amused.

The private room proved to be on the small side, and when Bingham and his son entered, they saw only a table and three chairs, two on the one side and a third on the other. They were still staring round, wondering where Raymond Dowdall might be when they heard the door locked behind them; at that moment, the young man entered through a door on the far side of the room, accompanied by a warder who took up his position in one corner. He then came forward and repeated what the original officer had said; nevertheless, Bingham, being of an old-fashioned disposition, stepped forward and shook the young man by the hand.

"Hello," he said in his most amiable voice, "I'm George Bingham and this is my son, Ben."

He stepped aside slightly, allowing Ben to move in and, also, shake Raymond Dowdall by the hand. Neither of the prison officers made so much as a move to prevent his courteous exchange.

The young man looked around for a moment and then moved quickly to straighten the three chairs, so they were set at right angles to the table and at an equidistance from it.

"I had a letter from my parents. They said you were coming," he said.

It was a bald statement, nothing more; in the prisoner's tone there was no indication that he held out any hopes as to the outcome of Bingham's visit. This was unusual in his experience: it was always another's hope of finding a loved one that brought Bingham into the picture. But then, how could one find lost years?

Bingham looked at the young man and thought he'd never seen a kinder or gentler face. The word 'resignation' sprang to mind. After fourteen years, Raymond Dowdall would be well institutionalised; half his life lived at home, looked after by his mother, and the other half looked after by the prison system.

Despite himself, Bingham began to feel drawn into the young man's problems. What if he was innocent? But why suppose such a possibility? Bingham knew this was a key moment in their relationship and in his own life: if he never saw the prisoner again, it would stick with him. He was at a loss as to how he might start the conversation, when Ben indicated that his father should take one of the chairs and sat down himself.

"You went to school with a friend of mine, didn't you, Raymond? Mervyn Ward?"

"Yes, I know Mervyn, but I've not seen him for a long time."

"My dad has helped several people by finding those they've lost, and Mervyn thought he might help you."

"I haven't lost anything."

"Mervyn believes you've lost fourteen years of your life."

"How can you lose years?"

Noting his son's puzzled expression, Bingham asked, "If, when you were a child, someone took away one of your toys, you might say you'd lost the toy, mightn't you?"

"Yes, I suppose so," replied Raymond, after some thought, "but it may not be lost. It might just be missing."

"But lost to you?"

"I didn't lose it. It was taken."

"You said 'missing'," replied Bingham, "What have you missed for fourteen years?"

"My mum and dad and my home."

"So, they've been lost to you – the years you've missed being at home, the lost years?"

Suddenly, Raymond Dowdall laughed as though cataracts had been removed from his eyes and he could see clearly.

"Lost years! I never thought of them in that way."

"No," replied Bingham, eager to gain some agreement, "Ben and I are here to see if we can help. We can't find those lost years, but we might be able to see that you don't lose any more."

Raymond Dowdall laughed, again, his mind now fixed on the expression Bingham had used. He could see the young man playing with the phrase, almost as though a new concept was forming in his mind.

"Raymond," he said, "Are you able – sorry, I mean *will* you tell us what happened on the day you found the lady's body? And do you mind if I make a few notes in my pocketbook? I'm an old man and I sometimes forget what people have said to me."

"I like the churchyard because I like old buildings and I always went there with my lunch. My mum always packed me the same lunch: corned beef sandwiches, a packet of crisps, an apple and a drink of fizzy orange. I like being alone there and looking out over the vale. Some people don't like churchyards because of the gravestones but they didn't frighten me. I felt at home there, and safe. It was this time of year; it was October and it was chilly, so I had my fleece on. Mum said I should wear it, even if the sun came out because the wind was cutting across the vale. Churches, you know, are always built so that they go east to west, and so the graveyard in on the north side and the north wind is cold.

Sometimes I see someone there: usually a lady walking her dog. She always speaks if she sees me. But I do not remember seeing her on that day, the day you want me talk about. But I did see a man. He came through the churchyard from the east, and he went by without speaking. He did not seem pleased to see me."

Bingham had to contain himself: desperate as he was to ask the obvious questions, he felt that interrupting the prisoner's flow would be nothing but destructive.

"I heard the clock strike when he passed. It was twelve o'clock. I had come out for my lunch early because we were not busy in the office, but we had a visit in the afternoon and Mr Roberts wanted me back early.

When I've finished my lunch, I sometimes walk round the church to have a look at the architecture. I like the buttresses and the parapets. The buttress is a projection from the church wall and is designed to give the wall additional strength and support. The weight of the roof and building tends to push the walls outwards, and so the buttresses strengthen them. Did you know that?"

"No," lied Bingham, pleased that he had a chance to manoeuvre Raymond's story back on track, "But go on – you got up to walk round the church," he continued, hoping this was the case.

"Yes, and I looked over the wall and saw a woman walking along the riverbank towards a copse of beech trees. I had never seen her before and so I did not need to speak, but she would not have heard me, anyway, because she was too far away."

"So, you walked round the church?"

"Yes – no, I watched the woman for a while because she seemed to be looking for someone. She was walking slowly. She was in no rush, and she kept looking behind her and from side to side, and, sometimes, she would look back from where she had come. I watched her until she disappeared into the coppice. Then, I went to look at the church architecture."

"You have a degree in architecture, don't you?" asked Ben.

"I do now. I did not then. But I have always been interested in old buildings. Mr Roberts gave me the job because I know a lot about old buildings. In Upton-on-Churnet there are lots of Victorian houses …"

"What happened when you got back to your seat?" asked Bingham, with a glance at his son.

Raymond Dowdall frowned at the interruption and a split second of anger flared in his eyes; one of his legs began to shake and he reached down to control the spasm. One of the warders stirred, but Bingham gave the officer a quick glance.

"I'm sorry to interrupt you, Raymond, but we only have a short time and you have more to tell us."

Raymond Dowdall blinked and shook his head, the shake making its way through his shoulders and along his arms. It was with a huge effort that he seemed to control himself.

"I saw the woman. She wasn't in the copse anymore but lying on the ground. Her legs were spread out, and she seemed to be twitching her arms. I thought she must have fallen but I did not see how. I went down to see if I could help her …"

"Just a moment," said Bingham, "I'm sorry to interrupt you again – really sorry, Raymond, and so please excuse my rudeness – but are you saying you went down to see if you could help her before you went back to your office to ask Mr Roberts to phone the police?"

"Yes."

"It's important to know that is so, you see, because I understood – sorry, was told – that you went straight back to your office."

"I would not do that, would I? I thought the woman had hurt herself."

"Yes, of course. Quite right. Go on."

"When I got close to her, I could see the blood. She was lying face down and so I turned her over to see if she was still alive. But first, I took off my fleece and put it to the side."

Bingham was desperate to ask why but frightened to interrupt.

"Her face was all right. There were no signs of injury but there was a lot of blood by the side of her head and her hair was soaked with it. I reached over to feel her pulse, and it was then that she sat up and shook her head.

There was a noise, but it was not the noise that made her sit up. She did not seem to hear the noise. She looked straight at me but did not see me. The noise came from the beech trees. I thought it was the wind rustling the leaves. And then she fell back again.

I picked up my jacket and ran to the office ..."

Raymond paused, and Bingham could see him struggling to remember something or someone. He glanced at his son, concerned that Ben should not interrupt the prisoner who seemed more than anxious to recall everything.

"It was Walter I saw on the way. He was standing by his white van. But I didn't talk to him. I ran up the road and back to the High Street. Our office is in the High Street and I knew Mr Roberts would be there because he always eats his lunch in the office. His wife packs him something different every day. Sometimes it's sandwiches and on other days it's buns. On some days she gives him an apple with a piece of cheese and on others she gives him grapes, and she puts different things in the sandwiches and buns, but I always have corned beef."

The young man looked across the table at Bingham. Was he talking too much? Was what he was telling them true? He knew it was, but did Bingham accept it as such. Bingham read these thoughts in the boy's mind; suddenly, he was a boy again. He had gone back fourteen years. In his working life, Bingham had handled lads like Raymond Dowdall. Back in the sixties, when Bingham started teaching, boys like Raymond would simply have been 'odd', and later in life they would have been called 'eccentric'. Nowadays, of course, they were given labels; labels might be useful, might show a greater understanding, although Bingham often wondered whether that was true, and he was averse to labels.

"Go on, son."

"Mr Roberts said we should go back to have a look before he phoned the police. I don't know why; he would not tell me. When we got back to the river, the woman had moved. She was on the footpath and not by the beech trees. Mr Roberts said that we should not touch her but wait for the police to arrive. He said he would also phone for an ambulance.

It was fifteen minutes before PC Boardman came. He came over to us and asked some questions. He asked who had found the woman and what I was doing by the river. He then went over to look at her and called me to him. He asked where I had found her, and I pointed to the place. He asked if I had touched anything and I said I had turned her over to see if she was still alive. It was then I noticed the blood on my hands, and I asked if I could wash them clean under the churchyard tap, but he said no: forensics would them as they were. He then placed his tunic over the body and made a phone call.

Twenty minutes later, another policeman arrived at the same time as the ambulance. He said he was Detective Inspector Oldman. I knew he was a detective because he was not in uniform. He asked me the same questions and I gave him the same answers. He made a phone call and then asked me if I was willing to go to the police station and answer some more questions. I sat in the back of the police car with one of the policemen and the other two sat in the front."

"What happened when you got to the police station, son?"

"I was taken to a room up some stairs. It was a big room with not much in it. There were two desks, five chairs and two filing cabinets. I was told to sit on one of the chairs and wait. PC Boardman left me there and Detective Inspector Oldman came in with another detective. Detective Inspector Oldman sat at the desk opposite me and the other man sat behind my left shoulder, and it made me feel uncomfortable. I do not like people sitting behind me. They took it in turns to ask me questions for fifteen minutes and then left the room. When they left, two policemen in uniform came in and watched me. When the detectives came back in, the two policemen left. This went on for a long time.

Sometimes, when the two policemen were there, PC Charlton came in and the other two went out. PC Charlton stood in front of me and looked at me. He was very friendly. He sounded like my dad. He said if I told the truth things would be easier for me. I asked him if I could see my dad and he said that there was no need because my mum and dad had been told where I was and that I was helping the police with their enquiries.

Later, my dad did come in with some clean clothes, and the police took my others that had the woman's blood on them ..."

"You say, 'later'," asked Bingham, unable to restrain himself, "What time was this?"

"It was dark outside. I could see that through the window. It was seven minutes past ten o'clock when I looked at my watch when dad asked me to take off my bloodstained clothes."

"Gentlemen, your time is up, I'm afraid."

It was one of the prison officers who spoke, cutting into Bingham's thought as he sat in what his son saw as a trance-like state. Ben had seen has father looking so, many times during the years he and his brother and sisters were growing up; it was usually when family discussions brought up past events and Bingham's mind roved back, lost in memories.

"Surely, we can have a few more minutes?" Ben insisted, "We've come a long way."

"I'm sorry, sir, but we have given you the full hour, despite your arriving late, and your time is up."

"Yes, yes," said Raymond, quickly, "We have sat here for a long time."

Bingham reached across and took the prisoner's right hand, clutching it with his own right and covering it with his left. The young man recoiled from his touch, but Bingham's hold was firm and his smile broad as he spoke.

"We'll be back, son – possibly not tomorrow, but we'll be back."

Ben followed his father's example as the far door opened and a third officer came for Raymond. Once the young man had disappeared from their sight, the door behind them opened and Bingham and his son were led back to the visitors' room and so from the prison.

At the final door, the officer who had first welcomed them took Bingham aside.

"Sorry about the abrupt ending, sir, but we have to be fair to one and all, and an hour for one is an hour for another – if you take my meaning. And, as you saw, Mr Dowdall had had enough."

"Of course," replied Bingham.

"For what it's worth, sir, and strictly off the record, none of us in here believe the young man to be capable of murder. In our experience, there are two types of lifers: those full of remorse for what they've done and those who keep insisting they didn't do it. Your Mr Dowdall doesn't fit the pattern. He never mentions it – never."

Chapter Two
LOOKING AT HIM HOSTILELY

Upton-on-Churnet in the autumn drizzle did nothing to lift Bingham's spirits when he and Ben stepped out of his son's car at the parking space in the rear yard of The White Hart. Ben had done the driving – much to Bingham's relief – and had woven his way through the misty rain along darkling roads, narrowly missing local vehicles that seemed to take mounting the verge as a matter of course and pedestrians who looked neither to right nor left as they shielded their faces from the rainwater that sprayed off every exposed surface: noticeboard, car, lamppost, pillar box. The small town – or was it a large village now that it no longer held a weekly market: Bingham wasn't sure – seemed to be a straggle of intertwining streets that twisted, curved and reared on the hillside. The stone-built houses, attractive, no doubt, in the summer sun, seemed only gloomy under a sullen sky that was sprinkling its load lightly and evenly.

"I'll take Mollie for a walk and then she'll settle," said Bingham, struggling from the car and helping the mongrel sheepdog to the ground. "I'll see if I can find some grass for her somewhere. She'll like that. It's more dignified."

"All right, Dad," replied Ben, "I'll get the cases inside and book us in. I'll have a pint ready for you when you get back."

"Thanks, Ben. That's good of you."

It had always been Bingham's way to see to the animals before anything else whenever the family arrived home, but Ben also knew that his father was tired, deep in thought and disinclined to talk. He wanted to be alone or, at least, alone with his dog.

Bingham made his way uphill from the public house, passed St Peter's Anglican church and out beyond its eastern wall until he came to the other church, St John the Baptist, the one that overlooked the Vale of the Churnet. Once free of the car and the possible pressure of his son's conversation (because, like his mother, Ben was a compulsive talker), Bingham begun to enjoy the rain. The fine precipitation settled gently on his coat and hair and stippled softly on his face. Mollie, too, seemed to sense the freedom of being out of the car and her tongue lapped lightly at the spots on the rough coat around her jaw. The walls of the church glistened in the wet, no longer dark but rather fresh, and the spray on the grass hung like morning dew.

Bingham had consulted the walking map his son bought with them and knew the Catholic church stood on the highest point of the village, overlooking the vale and beyond. It must have been from here that Raymond Dowdall sat each lunchtime, alone, enjoying the food his mother packed for him; and Bingham soon found the seat.

When he looked over the wall, Bingham was surprised at how inaccessible the riverside way seemed to be from the churchyard. Raymond Dowdall would have needed to take a narrow footpath down to New Road and followed this to where it joined the river. During this time, he would have lost sight of any occurrence on the riverside way itself. What had he said? 'When we got back to the river, the woman had moved.' Ah, but that was after he'd fetched Mr Roberts, wasn't it? Bingham consulted his notebook. Yes! Nevertheless, he would have lost sight of what might have been happening while making his way to the woman.

'The woman'! No one had mentioned her name; not only Raymond Dowdall himself, but also Ben and, presumably, Mervyn Ward. It was almost as though she existed only as the cause of a crime: the lost years of a young man's life. And yet, she was the victim of a murder. 'Come to know the victim and you are nearer solving the crime' someone had once said, and Bingham had no doubt the maxim was true.

"We need to make our way down, don't we, girl," he said to Mollie, catching sight of the dog looking up at him and realising this was the time of day she normally saw to her toilet.

Bingham looked at his watch. How long would it take? The path was narrow but not overgrown, suggesting its regular use by walkers, dog and others. The road itself was steep and wet with the drizzle and Bingham kept Mollie on the lead (unusually with her), realising they would stand no chance meeting a car on its way up.

It was only minutes, in fact, before they stood at the little crossroads where New Road became Longshaw Lane, Waggoner's Way bore off to his left and Bingham followed a wet path onto the riverside way. He unleashed Mollie and walked towards the copse of beech trees; part denuded, now, as autumn took them over.

The copse was an attractive place: in summer it would be dappled by the shimmering green leaves, in autumn their older selves crackled underfoot. Even on such a day, the ground beneath Bingham's feet was dry, the light rain having hung on the branches and the leaves that remained, yellow and golden. A romantic place to meet for those so inclined; a convenient place for a lunchtime tryst. Did 'the woman' come here regularly or was that one day, fourteen or fifteen years ago, a one-off encounter? Had Raymond Dowdall seen her before? Had he watched her meet a lover? Had he wondered, as any young man might?

Bingham looked back, keeping his eye on Mollie, and saw her select a spot. He waited until she'd finished and then took the plastic bag from his pocket. There was a bin at the end of the riverside walk (thoughtfully placed by the parish council, no doubt) and Bingham made for it.

'It was Walter I saw on the way. He was standing by his white van. But I didn't talk to him.' Where had the boy seen Walter? At the little crossroads? And what had Walter been doing, 'standing by his white van'? And who was Walter? Tomorrow would answer that question.

Bingham leaned on a wooden gate and gazed out across to where the Churnet wended its way along the vale. Trees lined the valley sides in places. It would be an attractive place for hiking – Toothill Wood, Moss Bank, the Churnet Way, Stoney Dale – but Bingham couldn't see Ben and himself doing much walking: not now, not now they'd met Raymond Dowdall.

"Come on, Mollie, let's get you dried off and fed. Hopefully there'll be a pint of Reverend James waiting for me. You can have your dinner and we can have a quiet sit together."

Ben had been better than his word: not only were their cases unloaded but Bingham's clothes were hung or stowed in their respective drawers in his room, where Mollie's bed was placed by the radiator. Ben knew his father's ways. Always on family holidays he had unpacked and settled his room before venturing anywhere. It had become a family joke, since his mother, Lina, was quite the opposite, already in conversation with the locals before Bingham appeared on the scene. He helped his father dry Mollie and settle him in the corner of the bar with the pint he'd mentioned.

"How did you know they'd have this particular pint on tap, Dad?"

"I know the area. Your mum and I brought you camping here, years ago. It's a Welsh beer, originally credited to the reverend himself who, I believe, ran a family brewery in Llanelli. Buckley, I think his name was. Saving souls and satisfying thirsts. Quite an achievement."

Their conversation drifted on in the way conversation does when people are comfortable in each other's company and have nothing to prove, each to the other. Ben could see his father meandering further into sleep – rather like Mollie, who rested her head on the old man's foot – and after a while he nodded to the barwoman, moved up to his room and came down a few minutes later wearing his hat and coat.

Over dinner, Bingham asked his son where he'd been.

"I hope you don't mind, Dad. I went to see Ray's parents."

"Why should I mind?"

"Did you know that one of your irritating habits is answering someone with a question."

"Your mother has mentioned it," laughed Bingham and continued, after a pause, "But it's pertinent, isn't it, to wonder why someone holds a particular thought? In this case, you clearly think I might mind you doing something that to me seemed perfectly normal."

"I thought you might consider that it could jeopardise our investigation."

"Your investigation, Ben. I came here for a walking break. I believe that's what you called it."

"But you believe, having spoken with him, that Raymond is innocent, don't you?"

"I don't believe anything, but if I was pushed for an opinion – having spoken with him, as you put it – I'd plump for the view that more likely than not he is guilty."

"Why?"

"He was a young man when Janet Bawley was murdered, and testosterone was, no doubt, pumping fiercely through his veins. Red-blooded they called it in my day. Suppose she'd met with a lover in that copse on more than that one occasion; suppose Raymond Dowdall had watched them from the spot he always ate his lunch. He'd be more than curious, wouldn't he? Suppose he went down there on that particular day ..."

"You're doing a lot of supposing, Dad."

"But none of it unreasonable – hmm? I don't know what happened any more than you. To do that we have to get into the mind of the victim – and in this case we have two … Did you notice his reaction when I interrupted what was about to become a diatribe on Victorian buildings?"

"He looked angry and began shaking."

"And one of the warders was about to intercept when I gave him a glance. I think your Mr Dowdall has a temper – how violent, I don't know, but certainly a temper. I'm wary of people with bad tempers, Ben."

"It's funny you should say that, Dad."

"You've spoken with his parents? Finish your starter before you tell me."

The White Hart served authentic Thai food on Thursday, Friday and Saturday evenings and Ben had begun with a starter of vegetable spring rolls with sweet chilli sauce and plum sauce, while Bingham had ordered only a main course, his seventy-five-year-old stomach now being satisfied with less food than previously. He sat enjoying his beer in gulps, waiting for his peaw waan (a sweet and sour dish with pineapple, cucumber, pepper and onion), while his son finished his first course.

Their main dishes arrived soon after and both men said little while they ate: Ben's meal was a sizzling stir-fry with herbs, almost the hottest dish on the menu: between eating, he spent his time cooling his mouth. It was as they sat after the meal, Ben with more beer and his father with a whisky, that he spoke of his visit to the Dowdalls.

"They believe Ray was framed for the murder. What he didn't mention was that the woman – by the way, how did you know her name?"

"I asked the young lady at the bar when I woke up," replied Bingham, "Go on."

"What Raymond didn't mention was that she was not dead when the ambulance came for her. Janet Bawley died a few days later in hospital. According to the Dowdalls, she was a promiscuous woman and had several local men – usually men with cash to spare – as lovers. Mr Dowdall gave me a long list and suggested that these influential men had conspired to keep their activities quiet by keeping Janet Bawley's promiscuity a secret.

He went on to say that several other characters were seen around the area on the day in question, but that these people – potential witnesses – had been warned off or ignored by the police. He mentioned a particular policeman – the neighbourhood bobby, I suppose – and said that this man had it in for Ray and coerced a confession from him.

Mrs Dowdall has a pile of newspaper cuttings and paperwork concerning attempts to get Ray out on appeal, but they'd all been unsuccessful. She said it was difficult speaking with Ray because his calls were monitored and restricted to a few minutes on his prison-issue phone card.

She was pleased when Ray got the job with Mr Roberts because it was one he enjoyed and would stick at; she was grateful to the estate agent who, she said, had been understanding and kind to Ray. He'd had difficulties at school, where he received special help, and found it hard to keep a job once he left. She said that people – neighbours – liked Ray. He was helpful, especially to old people and would tidy their gardens for them.

He was also good around the home, helping her with the housework. He liked everything in its place. He was a good cook, too, and very particular about measuring and timing.

He didn't go out much and had never had a girlfriend. He was a sharp dresser, she said, and listened to all the latest pop music but he hated discos and never went, even if someone he knew asked. Mrs Dowdall said he found it difficult to understand girls, in particular: they would tease him and get him to fetch a carry for them, and he never understood why they laughed at him. He found it difficult keeping up a conversation with them but liked their company.

The Dowdalls said he'd found prison life very difficult at first, especially being put in a cell with another prisoner. He attacked the man and had to spend time in solitary, which he preferred. Eventually, the authorities gave him his own cell, and once he'd settled to the routine of prison life, he seemed to enjoy it – something his parents found worrying and difficult to accept.

I think that's about it, Dad. They said they'd like to have a chat with you."

"Yes, well your visit's been most useful. We now have several local men who may – or may not – have been involved with Janet Bawley and several people who may – or may not – be witnesses on the day."

"You sound very sceptical, Dad. I realise the list of 'involved' men may just be the result of gossip – people sympathetic to the Dowdalls who wanted to feel they were helping but ..."

"No, no, Ben! I'm tired, not sceptical. You're right: never underrate gossip, so long as you sift the wheat from the chaff. And these 'potential witnesses' are important, too – who are they? Were they interviewed by the police at the time?"

"When will you see the Dowdalls?"

"You sound like your mother: you share her persistent nature," replied Bingham with a laugh as he stood up from their table. "Now – I'll drop by when I take Mollie for her last walk."

"Would you like a cup of tea, Mr Bingham?" asked Roberta Dowdall, when she'd ushered him into her best room and petted Mollie.

"That's very kind of you, Mrs Dowdall. It's a bleak, autumn night and a nice cup of hot tea will be just the job," replied Bingham, wondering how Raymond Dowdall would view his answer: it was, after all, a lie. Having drunk his fair share of beer the last thing Bingham wanted was a cup of tea. He rather fancied that the young prisoner would have difficulty understanding the nature of social lies.

"Call me Bobby, please."

Bingham disliked using a masculine version of their real names when addressing women. He was unsure why. He smiled as Bobby drew him to the chair closest to the fire. It was a cosy, little room with everything in its proper place. On the mantlepiece were photographs of their son at different ages: none after the age of seventeen. Bingham sensed the desperation of these parents and felt their sadness.

Bobby was a small woman with a smooth, rounded face. Bingham guessed her to be in her early fifties and thought that she probably looked much the same when she was twenty-something. It was the kind of face, and she the kind of personality, that was ageless. She reminded Bingham of her son: both shared the same cheerfulness. Bingham couldn't imagine that Roberta

Dowdall had ever lost her temper with Raymond, which he thought was fortunate.

"Sam is seeing to the locking up," said Bobby, "He won't be moment."

Raymond's father came in from the door that opened on to the kitchen. He brought the cold and damp of the night with him. It was obvious that he'd not only checked the windows but also the back gate and any outhouses. Sam Dowdall was also short but with a sharp face – one that would at one time have been called foxy – and he fixed Bingham with a wary eye. There was a nervousness about his manner that might have made a stranger feel ill at ease.

"Mr Bingham," he said, extending his hand, "I'm pleased you've come, although we didn't expect you to turn out this late at night."

"We ought to make Mr Bingham welcome, Sam," urged his wife.

"Of course, of course – and you are, sir, believe me."

Watching the two parents, Bingham realised that it was the man who bore the brunt of their son's imprisonment, shouldering not only his own anger and sadness but also the worries of his wife: she was a woman who would fret, constantly.

"Please call me George. You told my son a great deal, and I don't want you to feel you have to go over that ground again …"

"George, we've been over that ground thousands of times, and are only too happy to go over it again," interrupted Sam.

"I would like you to tell me about that day fourteen years ago. Anything you can remember. Any small detail."

This was Bingham at his most courteous: not wishing to show a lack of interest in Raymond, about whom he felt he'd heard enough for one day, he asked about *that* morning; what he really wanted was a picture of the small town.

"The first we knew of it was when one of the coppers knocked on our door. I'd just returned from work and Bobby was getting the tea on. He said that Raymond was being held at the police station for questioning in connection with an assault on a young woman. You can imagine how we felt at hearing that news. He said it was likely they'd be in touch later in the day."

"This would be at about six o'clock, would it?"

"Yes – as I said, Bobby was getting the tea on. I asked if the boy needed a solicitor and the copper said no: they were only asking him questions. Later, when we heard that the young woman had been attacked at midday, I did think it strange that Raymond was still being question six hours later.

We were on tenterhooks all evening until about ten o'clock when another copper called, asking us to take Raymond some fresh clothes. He was in a hell of a state when I got there. He said he was cold and tired and that he'd had nothing to eat since lunchtime. I asked him where he'd been and he said, 'Here in this room'. 'What, all the time,' I said, and he said 'Yes'. He took off the clothes he was wearing, and I saw they had blood on them …"

"Where?"

"On the knees and there were splashes on his shirt and on the inside of the fleece he was wearing when he went to work. He'd had some on his hands as well, but they wouldn't let him wash them until the forensic people had taken samples.

I asked him what had happened but there was a copper in the room – a local bloke: Charlton – and he said we couldn't talk about what happened. We only had ten minutes together at the most. I had the impression they were keen to get rid of me and had only called me in because they wanted Raymond's bloodstained clothes. We learned later that he made a statement soon after I left to find a solicitor – not the easiest of tasks, eleven o'clock at night. Have you seen the statement, George?"

"No."

"We have a copy."

"Later will do, Sam. I want your impressions, first," replied Bingham, eager to steer the conversation in another direction. You gave my son a list of names."

"Janet Bawley's fancy men!" snapped Bobby.

"Yes, and you mentioned that several people were in the neighbourhood of the footpath during that lunch hour. I'd like to know what each of these people was doing at that time and where they were."

"It's only what people have told us," said Bobby.

"The people on the list are just names to me; to you they are neighbours."

"Well," replied Bobby, "we could start with James Cummings ..."

Bingham eased himself back in the chair by the fire. This was what he'd turned out on a wet, autumn evening to hear. For the next hour he said nothing, although he made notes, while Bobby Dowdall did all the talking.

It was as he rose to leave, long past his usual bedtime, that Sam Dowdall spoke.

"Would you like to see Raymond's clothing?" asked Bobby.

"I'm sorry?"

"We have the clothes Raymond was wearing that day. They were sent back to us after the forensic people had tested them."

Sam Dowdall left the fireside at a nod from his wife and returned a few seconds later holding a small drawer he had obviously pulled from a chest. It contained Raymond's work clothes: a pair of smart black trousers, a white shirt, a floral tie, a pair of black shoes, the fleece and a wristwatch with a leather strap.

Bingham touched the clothes gingerly: not because the bloodstains made him nervous but rather because he realised the items were mementoes, precious to these parents. There were splashes of blood on the front of the shirt and on the tie. These had been highlighted with a forensic marker otherwise Bingham would have missed them against the floral design. There was a deep stain on the right knee of the trousers and what appeared to be a footprint on the inside of the fleece.

"These clothes of Raymond's are hardly drenched in blood, are they, George?" said Sam, "and yet he's supposed to have battered the young woman to death with a fallen branch. If he'd done that surely his clothes would have been covered in blood, wouldn't they?"

Bingham didn't answer; he wasn't one to offer an opinion about something of which he knew nothing. How did blood spill from a wound brought about by battering? Besides, it was the first he'd heard of how Janet Bawley had been murdered and he was shocked.

"Do I remember your son saying that when he got back to the riverside path with Mr Roberts the young woman had moved?

"Yes, yes, that's in his statement," replied Bobby, "We have a pile of paperwork from Raymond's appeal. I'll fetch it."

"No, no," said Bingham, "I'll come back and look through all of it when I'm fresh in the morning. I'll bring my son with me. He has a way with paperwork. You've ... hmm ... given me much to think about. Thank you."

When Bingham left the Dowdalls he felt drained of all emotion and intelligence and wondered how professional police officers (for whom he had the greatest respect) coped with such an investigation. The sight of the bloodstained clothes had been appalling enough, but the knowledge of how Janet Bawley met her death struck home with an even greater ferocity. His friend, ex DCI Simon Brockie, had once told him that a form of black humour peculiar to the job was the only defence; this was the same Brockie who had felt sickened when he cracked a suspect's head against a lamppost when arresting him. 'He was the only villain I ever hurt, George, in all my years as a copper'.

It was touching midnight when Bingham walked back to The White Hart. The rain had stopped but a sullen, autumn mist obscured his view and bemused his memory of the way to what would be home for the next week. He remembered the post office was to his right before he turned into the High Street and before this there should be a strange building referred to as the Round House. He seemed to have come about in a circle from the Dowdall's home. 'A straggle of intertwining streets': his own thoughts on their arrival returned to him as he realised that he was lost. He'd never panicked before, not ever, even when crossing strange moorland in the dark, but he felt uneasy here in this little market town. As if to add to his sense of apprehension, the streetlamps died: no doubt an economy of the local council.

His eyes no longer young, Bingham was careful where he trod, concerned about stumbling and twisting his ankle should he slip off the edge of a curb. The pavements were still damp underfoot and glistened in the light of the almost full moon, which had risen as he set out for the Dowdalls. The walls of the shops and houses, too, caught the moon's bright, yellow light. Fine droplets of the afternoon's rain fell from the one or two hedges that fenced off some of the stone-built house from the road. He became aware of the smell of smoke, woodsmoke from chimneys where early fires had burned in the grates that evening.

Mollie, loose by his side, twitched, glanced behind her but stayed close. He was relieved when, eventually, he saw the Round House and across the road the white walls of a cottage he noticed as his son drove past. Ahead would be a post box in the wall, its surface gleaming in the moonlight.

He looked down to see what was bothering Mollie when another kind of smoke invaded his nostrils: the sour smell of a cigarette. A voice said:

"Don't turn around, Mr Bingham. We just want a word. That's all."

Something with a round end was thrust into his back. Mollie turned and snarled. The round object was removed suddenly, and Bingham feared the worst. He turned. A man in a balaclava was pointing a rounded stick, somewhat narrower than a broom handle at Bingham's dog. He raised it to strike.

"Leave her alone," said Bingham, "She was startled. That's all. You must have come upon us suddenly. What can I do for you?"

The eyes behind the mask peered at Bingham, who couldn't see their colour but read their intent, looking at him hostilely as they did.

"I told you not to turn around! It's what we can do for you, Mr Bingham, that matters. We can give you a warning for the good of your health. Keep your fucking nose out of the Dowdall business. Do you understand?"

"More or less but what concern is it of yours?"

"Never you mind. Just stay clear. It's good advice," replied the man, raising the stick once again as though he would thump Bingham on the chest; instead, thinking better of his intention, he turned and ran off in the direction of The White Hart, finally disappearing into an alley.

Mollie looked at Bingham, the expression on her face asking: 'what was all that about?' Bingham smiled and ruffled her ears. First the Dowdalls and now his would-be assailant: he'd learned a great deal from both.

Chapter Three
THREE NEW WITNESSES

"I'm going for a haircut," said Bingham, as he and Ben sat eating their breakfasts the following morning.

It was a good breakfast at The White Hart: Ben with his Full English, Bingham with two poached eggs on toast and a decent cup of tea. You could always rely on that in Britain. While they waited for their repast to be cooked fresh, Bingham had relayed the events of the previous night.

"Do you think the youth was sent to frighten us off, Dad, or was he ..."

"... acting on his own accord?" continued Bingham, "And who ..."

"... could have put him up to it, if he was ..."

"... sent as a warning? Just about anyone we've spoken to, I suppose, but they've moved quickly. We've only been ..."

"... here the one night," Ben said, completing Bingham's sentence with a laugh.

"What's funny?" asked Bingham, knowing full well what had amused his son.

As a boy, Bingham had been brought up by his solicitor father and musician mother – both of whom had strict (some would say 'middle-class' attitudes to good manners) – never to interrupt another person

40

when they were speaking. In this way, Bingham had grown up listening to ideas expounded at length with time to reflect on what was being said; it had also enabled him to formulate a response, knowing his ideas would be heard in full. It was a mode of speaking in company that produced conversation as distinct from chatter.

When he and Lina married that changed completely: she had been raised in a family where talking was continuous, one subject spinning off another with no apparent connection between each other than the speaker's desire to speak. It was Lina's style of conversing that caught on in the family, however, and dominated their lives together. This was especially true when their daughters were around; only when alone with one of his sons did Bingham find the space to cogitate and appreciate the silence between thoughts.

Even then, the habits of the fireside and meal table were hard to shake off; this had irritated Bingham and still did, but in such company the only way to be heard was to interrupt and he had descended into what he considered to be rudeness.

"You know very well what's funny, Dad."

"Let's make a silent promise to each other, shall we?"

"Agreed. Why the hairdressers?"

"Janet Bawley worked there. If gossip reached the youth who threatened me, it's likely to have reached the ladies at The Old Stables Hairdressing. It's a nice-looking place and has a good reputation."

Bingham wasn't a vain man but was fussy about his hair and always kept to the same salon in Ipswich, his memories of the enforced horrors of a 'short-back-and-sides' as a child being indelibly printed in his psyche:

once you find a good hairdresser, stay with them was his motto. Knowing this and the teasing his father had undergone from his mother and sisters, Ben laughed.

"What do you want me to do?" he asked.

"Have a sniff around and see what you can find. We've uncovered a great deal already. We need to contact your friend, Mervyn Ward: find out if he's here, and if not get him.

Ask around about Walter and his white van; he's probably a local – or was at the time – and possibly in business here.

Ask our young barwoman if she knows the youth; she may be the source of the gossip that brought him to me.

Run down the list of Janet Bawley's lovers and see if you can locate any of them – also those people around the footpath at the time; the names are in my notebook.

Mr Roberts – no leave him to me.

See if you can bump into any of the Dowdall's neighbours and ask about Raymond.

Girls – they'll be young women, now – who knew him; they'll be a mine of information. I'll probably come across them at the hairdressers.

Charlton – yes – the copper who was with Raymond when Sam Dowdall took in the change of clothes; be careful with him: locating him might be enough. He could well be retired by now.

Ooh, and blood; give Paul a ring – he's less snappy with you than with me – and ask about blood loss in anyone battered almost to death with a branch.

And the youth – we can't miss him. It was a mistake him threatening me. Not that he was to know that."

"Anything else?"

"Hmm?"

"Anything else? I'll have plenty of time to cover that lot, while you're getting your hair cut."

"There's no need for sarcasm, Ben. Be selective. Start with the youth. He's not local but presumably lives here, and that could be because he works here. He ..."

"How do you know he's not local?"

"He comes from Walsall," replied Bingham with a smile.

"How do you know?"

"I was born and raised in Wolverhampton, wasn't I? I can tell by their accent whether a Midlander is from Dudley, Walsall, Stafford, Tamworth, Leek, Eccleshall, Cannock ... Do you want me to go on? His dress was undistinguished: the usual jeans, trainers and what we used to call a windcheater – fake leather, I was pleased to see – but he's a Wolves supporter. There may not be many of them in Upton: I think they favour Stoke, round here.

And he smokes untipped cigarettes – unusual, I'd have thought. I've seen these kids roll their own and put the filter tip in place. But these were bought cigarettes. I don't know what brands they still make: Woodbines, Senior Service, Players, Park Drive ...? I wouldn't know but they won't be cheap ...

Oh, and he's short – no more than five foot six – and thin. He had his face covered but the eyes were dark, I'm sure – probably brown. And his hands were grubby. Take Mollie with you. She'll recognise him by his smell."

The Old Stables Hairdressing was all Bingham imagine it to be as he strolled down Queen's Walk from

Dray Bank. The weather had cleared after a blustery autumn night when the wind had shaken his window and he'd listened to the rain pelting down on the roof of the public house. But the morning was bright and fresh. Heavy rain had washed clean every surface and each now sparkled in the sun. Bingham loved autumn: the yellow and the golds of the trees, the sharp gleam of the sun, the peace of the season and the nip in the air that called people to the hearth. It was a time when the earth seemed to retreat into itself, recuperating, building its strength for the coming of winter, protecting its yet-to-be-born for the following spring, the time of rebirth.

The stone walls of the village were alive with moss, hanging ivy and ferns that seemed to sprout from the rock itself, clinging precariously to vertical surfaces, glistening now with the night's wetting.

He didn't have to wait, even for a moment: experience had taught Bingham to arrive early and he found a chair waiting and a girl ready. He explained when asked that he liked his hair 'soft on the ears', a phrase he'd picked up from the Ipswich salon, and stressed that he wanted no more than half-an-inch removed all-over and, yes, he 'preferred a scissor cut'. He had no idea what the alternative might be but the idea of an electric shaver being run from his neck upwards leaving him looking like a crested canary held no attraction.

Hairdressers have incredible memories: he knew that to be true by the amount of detail the young women back home remembered from previous visits. Memory of that kind only grows from asking the right questions and having a sharp ear for gossip. His current cutter had soon elicited that he was a stranger, a friend of a friend of Raymond Dowdall, was on a walking break with his son, was staying at the community pub, had met Raymond's parents and taken a look at where he was supposed to have killed the young woman.

"Supposed?" asked Bingham.

"No one believes he did it," replied the girl. "He was too stupid to kill anyone. He didn't have it in him."

"Did you know him?" asked Bingham, realising the girl could only have been six or seven when Raymond was sent to prison.

"One of the older women knew Janet Bawley. She was a friend of hers. She only works on a Friday and Saturday now, when we're busy. She'll be in later. Lauren sees to her mother first. She says she still thinks about it and how shocked the town was at the time. Things like that don't happen in Upton. Everyone knows one another and so we notice strangers in a place like this."

"And there were strangers in the town on that day?"

"There was a man got off the early bus. One of the customers noticed him because he was only wearing a T-shirt and it was a cold day – like today. Everyone else had coats on. He got off the bus and walked backwards and forwards looking at his watch and then he went off towards the river."

"And Lauren remembers this?"

"No, not Lauren. Mrs Wright. She's elderly, now, of course, but she still has her hair done once a week. It's very thin but it keeps her looking smart."

"And he definitely got off the bus?"

"So, she says, and later she saw him up at the Catholic church wandering around and then down by the river talking to Walter."

"Did Mrs Wright say how old this man appeared to be? Could she describe him?"

"She said he was middle-aged – about forty or forty-five – and was on the bulky side."

"Who is this Walter?"

"He's a painter and decorator – an odd job man, really. He'll turn his hand to anything. He decorated this salon for us only last year. Made a good job, didn't he?"

The décor of the salon was certainly smart: veneered chipboard lined most walls, offset by mirrors on all sides, and this was matched by the floorboards, giving an overall rustic effect both homely and practical. The ceiling and other walls were painted a sheer, matt white with not a brushstroke in sight. The many electric sockets were neatly placed and horizontally aligned with each other. It was a prefabricated job but carried out by someone with pride in his work.

"Yes, he did a good job" replied Bingham, "Does Walter live in the village?"

"He works from home. His wife is one of our customers, isn't she, Doth?"

Doth, which Bingham took as a pet name contracted from Dorothy, had walked in a few minutes before, in a hurry, embarrassed to be late but now ready for her first customer, an elderly woman who sat patiently waiting and listening to Bingham's conversation with his cutter whose name he hadn't liked to ask but was about to discover.

"That's right, Glenda. Milly comes in once a month for her highlights to be done."

"We all saw him," said the elderly lady who was now being attended to by Doth, "I was shaking out the mats when he got off the bus, and he definitely went down to the river. Later, Mrs Shaws saw Raymond Dowdall running back through the town. That would have been at lunchtime because she was at the shop getting what she needed for her husband's dinner."

"You must have told this to the police at the time," suggested Bingham.

"They never asked."

"They must have made house to house enquiries."

"Mrs Wright did go to the police station, didn't she?" Glenda replied, "I remember her saying so."

"Mrs Shaws did, too. She said she made a statement and was told not to tell anyone or talk about it to anyone else."

"Mrs Wright said they didn't seem interested."

"They knew who'd done it by then," said the elderly lady, pursing her lips and drawing in breath knowingly.

Bingham felt lost among the gossip and sympathised, belatedly, with the police officers who were challenged into sorting truth from falsehood, evidence from chatter, the germane from the irrelevant. As he tried to sift through the sequence of events, he heard the bell on the salon door ting and looked up.

The woman in the doorway, who must have overheard the final remarks as she entered, was an attractive person somewhere in her mid-forties. He knew at once that this was Lauren: knew by her manner as she looked around the salon and her bearing, which suggested she had an opinion on the matter under discussion, an opinion based on more than rumour and hearsay. She smiled but said nothing and passed quickly through the salon to where the hairdressers must have kept their personal belongings because she arrived back a few minutes later in a smart tunic and began setting up her station.

No sooner had she finished than another customer arrived, smiled at everyone and walked straight to where Lauren was waiting.

"I thought I'd caught you then, Lauren," she said, "I saw you come out of the post office. I could see you were running late. How's your mother?"

"She's fine, Mrs Dawkins, thank you. The usual?"

"Yes please, dear. Just tidy me up."

"We were just talking about Janet Bawley's murder," said Lauren, "Or rather that was the topic of conversation when I came in. Your Maureen had some doings with the appeal, didn't she?"

"The judge said her evidence was inadmissible," replied Mrs Dawkins, "She swore she'd seen a couple kissing and cuddling down by the river. Of course, she was only a teenager at the time and frightened to come forward. The judge said that as she hadn't come forward at the time her 'evidence was no longer credible'. I'll never forget him saying that – that phrase stuck in my mind – 'evidence was no longer credible'. It was as though he thought our Maureen was making it up. She's nearly the same age as poor Janet Bawley, now, and with children of her own."

Lauren looked at Bingham while Mrs Dawkins was speaking, looked at him hard and meaningfully; and he knew she was provoking further conversation deliberately for his benefit. So, she had been Janet Bawley's friend, had she?

"Is that what you wanted?" asked Glenda, holding up a mirror behind Bingham so that he might inspect her handiwork on the back of his head; and he knew his time was up.

"Enjoy your walk!" a chorus of voices sent him on his way, and he wondered how in the time it took him to pay Glenda and struggle into his coat the women had all come to know he was on a walking holiday.

Bingham was disappointed to be leaving because he knew the conversation around Raymond Dowdall would continue but he, at least, had two new witnesses: Mrs Wright with her stranger from the bus and Maureen Dawkins who'd seen a couple kissing on the river path. He also now knew that Walter the handyman lived in the village and that Lauren had been a close friend of the murdered woman. Somehow, he knew she'd be in touch.

The sun was now up. Across a clear, blue sky scudded a few fluffy clouds: cumulus but light and threatening no rain. Queen's Walk had dried out and Bingham walked steadily, hugging the stone wall to his right because there was no footpath. The houses on either side were stone-built as were the walls, the latter often laid without cement, leaning inwards, resting on the earth. To one side, a man was cutting a privet hedge, to the other a Leylandii hedge rose, tall and unnatural, Bingham thought, in gardens dominated by ferns, moss and the lovely trunks of the silver birch.

Outside the Londis store on Dray Bank, a few locals stood chatting, smiled at Bingham as he passed, and he wondered how long it would be before the whole village knew what he and his son were about. A little further on he passed the post office to his right, where the youth from Walsall had threatened him the previous evening and came to the junction with the High Street and the New Road, which went down to the river.

Bingham paused for a moment, seeing for the first time in daylight the road up which Raymond Dowdall would have had to run bearing his message for Mr Roberts. Making a mental note to take the same track later in the morning, Bingham continued to the estate agents, a small property on the left of the street that would have felt quite comfortable in a film of one of Dickens's novels. P R Roberts and Sons, Estate Agents – Surveyors – Auctioneers was a property typical of the houses along the street with a cottage window and a low door recessed in the wall. The black and white paintwork was fresh, covering wooden frames that gave the impression of having seen better days, but this only added to the charm of the place. Leaning back against the iron railings, which offered some protection from passing traffic, Bingham felt he might be about to lurch forward into history. He felt it even more so when he opened the door, a bell rang, and he was obliged to step down into the office.

A fat girl with a round face and a broad smile explained that Mr Roberts was "busy at present" but if Bingham would "care to wait" she would "let Mr Roberts know you are here" and "would you like a cup of tea". She was as unhurried as the feel of the village suggested she might be, and Bingham didn't like to refuse the tea, lest the young woman was offended, although he'd rather have waited for coffee.

As it turned out, Mr Roberts, hearing Bingham's name, arrived before the young woman, who her employer addressed as 'Emily', could make the drink.

"Mr Bingham. I recognise you, sir, from your photo in the newspapers. How long ago was it, now? Four years! Doesn't time fly? It doesn't seem possible. Four years! What a wonderful achievement that was, sir – rounding up that paedophile gang."

"I didn't actually round up any gang, Mr Roberts: the police did ..."

"But only after you'd set them on the right track, Mr Bingham."

So much for newspapers and impression they create, thought Bingham. He'd tried to avoid publicity following his first case but the subsequent investigation by the Paedophile Unit at Scotland Yard had brought the press to his door.

"I can guess why you're here, sir. You're after getting Raymond released ..."

"I ..."

"Mr and Mrs Dowdall were round this morning, Mr Bingham. They've every confidence in you and your son. Emily, pop along to the Londis and see if they have some doughnuts for Mr Bingham – fresh, mind, we don't want to offer yesterday's doughnuts to our guest, do we now! And coffee! Get some coffee on, there's a good girl."

Bingham smiled at Emily. He'd never worked in an establishment where women were ordered about and he felt embarrassed, but Emily smiled back, grabbed her coat from a rack that stood behind the small door and scooted off.

"Sit down, Mr Bingham, sit down, sir, and fire away," chortled Mr Roberts, as he pulled back the chair usually reserved for clients, a padded wooden chair with arms that surrounded the sitter, and ushered Bingham into it.

"If you'd just run over the events of that morning, Mr Roberts," said Bingham, hurriedly, eager to stop the man talking further and omitting the usual invitation to use his first name, in case the estate agent inferred they were on familiar terms.

Mr Roberts did as he was asked at length. Before he'd finished, Emily had arrived with the doughnuts and brewed the coffee; but Bingham sat quietly, listening and watching Raymond Dowdall's employer.

"When you arrived at the riverbank, did you see a man called Walter by his white van?"

"Walter Higgins, you mean. No. Raymond said he was there, afterwards, but he'd gone by the time we arrived."

"Do you know the man?"

"He's well-known in the town. A good craftsman. He does work for us occasionally."

"Where will I find him?"

Mr Roberts leaned forward and wrote an address neatly and with great care onto a pad. He then tore off the sheet and handed it to Bingham as though he was passing across a document of great confidentiality.

"Why did you take on Raymond Dowdall?"

Mr Roberts smiled, pleased to be asked the question.

"Raymond had had difficulties holding down a job once he'd left school. It was a pleasure to help. Besides, I liked the lad. Mrs Roberts and I have no children. I know – the sign over the door says 'P R Roberts and Sons'. I'm one of the sons. P R was my father. Peter Rupert after our grandfather. He started the business. My brothers and I kept it going. Our main office is in

Stoke. My older brother – he's Peter, I'm Rupert – runs that one and my younger brother is an accountant who works in Hanley. This is only a small office but – we like to believe – a select one. As I say, Raymond is like a son to me – and he knows his buildings. Very impressed the clients are when Raymond holds forth: they like to know they are getting their money's worth. Some of the buildings in Upton date back to Tudor times and there's nothing Raymond doesn't know about old buildings ..."

Bingham realised he was almost not listening; he'd drifted back into his own feelings at forty when he, too, thought he might face life without children. But then he'd met Lina and the world had changed. He found himself drawn to Mr Roberts.

"Was he punctual?"

"On the dot. He never walked through that door before nine o'clock and he never walked through that door a second after nine o'clock. It was the same with his lunch: on the stroke of noon, he was off. When I asked him to go early ..."

"As you did on that day."

"Yes ... he was quite perplexed. It took me a while to persuade him that we needed to start our afternoon earlier than usual because we had a client arriving at 1 o'clock."

"But, usually, you had no difficulty working with him?"

"He could be difficult, but you must understand that Raymond had his problems."

"Did he ever show any signs of violence?"

"I'm not sure I like the question, Mr Bingham. If you're inferring Raymond might have killed that young woman in an outburst of rage I must protest, sir, I really must."

The estate agent sat up in his chair and bristled, curling his lip and glaring at Bingham. He sniffed, as though to emphasise his disapproval at what he took to be a presumption.

"I'm inferring nothing, Mr Roberts, but your reaction suggests he did."

"He could become ... shall we say, agitated."

"With clients?"

"At first, when they interrupted his flow. But he and I reached an understanding. I would indicate with a movement of my hand that what he'd said was sufficient to interest the client and that he was to pause for questions."

"And he did?"

"More than that Mr Bingham: it became a standard practice between us. Raymond took a real delight in the gesture."

"And became quite agitated when an occasion no longer called for it?"

"Yes," replied Mr Roberts, sharply, "You are persistent, Mr Bingham."

"So, people tell me. There's no point in avoiding possibilities, Mr Roberts. We have to eliminate those ..."

"So that whatever remains, however improbable, must be the truth," said the estate agent, reducing himself to a chortling, shaking bundle as offered the much-shared quote from Conan Doyle.

"Something like that," replied Bingham, with a smile, pleased that they were, once again, on friendly terms. "What did you make of the scene on the riverbank?"

"Make of it?"

"You stood waiting for the police for some time. What were your impressions while you waited and when they arrived?"

"They took their time," replied the estate agent, responding much as Bingham anticipated, which led him nicely into what he wanted to know.

"Just as Raymond said. It must have been an anxious time for him."

"Yes, he was very quiet."

"He must have wanted to cut himself off from it."

"Yes, he finds emotion difficult to handle and we were all very upset at seeing the young woman lying there in that way."

"For Raymond that must have been particularly stressful. I imagine he was very withdrawn."

"That's exactly how I would describe him, Mr Bingham. It was almost as though he wasn't there."

"Natural enough, as you say. He could make neither head nor tail of what was going on around him and so he withdrew into himself. How did he react when the police officer asked him to accompany them to the station?"

"He was bewildered, Mr Bingham. He got into the police car like a sleepwalker."

"Did he say much while you waited for the police to arrive?"

"Almost nothing."

"He never mentioned seeing a man walk through the churchyard while he was eating his lunch?"

"No, and nor has he since when I have visited him."

"Does he ever mention that day?"

"No, it's as though he has shut it away completely."

"You've been very helpful, Mr Roberts. I'd like to think that I might talk with you again."

"Of course, Mr Bingham – if there's anything I can say or do, I'll be only too pleased to be of assistance."

"If you don't mind, I'd now like to clear my own head. I need to take a walk. You've given me a great deal to think about. Thank you and your receptionist for the coffee and the doughnuts."

"Our pleasure, Mr Bingham, our pleasure. Our little agency is at your disposal at any time, sir. If we can be of any help at all in freeing this young man, nothing will be too much trouble. I take it, sir, he has spoken to you. But of course, of course! He would, wouldn't he" replied Mr Roberts, regaining his garrulous style of speech.

Bingham gave Emily a smile as he passed through the outer office. Mr Roberts showed him to the little door in the recess, urging him to:

"Mind the step. We always remind our clients to 'mind the step'. We don't want any of them falling into the street, now do we?"

He seemed as pleased following his conversation with Bingham as he would have done following a successful sale.

'Bewildered' was the key word Bingham carried away with him as he made his way up the High Street, avoiding the hazard of the stepped curb, which seemed designed to protect the narrow footpath from the road. Raymond Dowdall found extreme difficultly interpreting what others were thinking or saying; facial expressions, body language, social cues meant nothing to him, and he would have trouble keeping up with a conversation. The trouble is, thought Bingham, if you cannot order your own thoughts, there are others will do the job for you. Two witnesses? No, in less than a morning, he'd unearthed three witnesses, although it might be a challenge talking with the third.

Chapter Four

THE UNCHARITABLE THOUGHT

Much as it would have surprised Lina, Bingham had not forgotten to take his phone with him that morning and decided he would contact his son, but not yet: he did need to clear his head. He looked up at the sky: an action born of habit. Would it rain today, as it had when they arrived? Not for a while, although small clouds, some stratus, were gathering, small but threatening.

Bingham turned the corner and began his descent of New Road, retracing the flight of Raymond Dowdall on that awful day fourteen or so years ago. It was a pleasant enough walk on such a morning. Bingham reached the one footpath, which began at the Methodist church on his right. The church stood higher than the road, shielded from the footpath by a stone wall and railings topped with Victorian spears that Bingham, as a one-time teacher, considered so dangerous for children, inclined, as they were, to climbing; to his left, on the far side of the road, there was only a grass verge. He passed a small cottage of the type considered traditionally English, fronted by a dainty porch, also guarded from the road by similar railings. On either side, growing securely above stone walls, were beautifully manicured privet hedges.

Ahead there was the vale. As he turned the corner, Bingham was surrounded on either side by natural woodlands, their spread controlled by more stone walls. Here, the footpath, which had disappeared for a brief time, reappeared on the other side and Bingham crossed over, noting that he might find 'traffic in the middle of the road'.

Ivy shrouded the walls, its dominance broken in places by the cleanest, most lustrous ferns Bingham had ever seen; it was dark under the trees, despite the sun shining brightly through the leaves, silhouetting the trunks. To his left a steep bank declined to the floor of the vale. Further along, the stone wall was replaced by a higher one of concrete, a wall under pressure as the surrounding trees leaned heavily against it.

He came to the junction and the beauty of his surroundings was driven out by the realisation of where he stood: the crossroads. It was here so much must have occurred on the morning Janet Bawley was murdered. Bingham kept returning to that thought. His son had brought him to Upton because he felt the friend of a friend had been wrongly convicted of her murder; but she was the first victim, and if the conviction was wrong Janet Bawley had never received justice.

Bingham looked around. A brown, tourist notice informed him that the 'Ramblers Rest' was to his left. Also, to his left, along Waggoner's Way, was the Upton Bridge Hotel and 'The Tolbooth', an eighteenth-century inn, according to the dark blue sign with the rampant lions. And to his right, the lane: the lane that led to the copse of beech trees, the lane along which Raymond Dowdall had run in both directions, firstly to see if he could help the stricken woman and, secondly, to seek his employer.

This was a busy crossroads: busy, that is, for a one-time market town at midday. Walkers, retired locals, people on business trips and those who worked in the town would be making their way to the pub or other eatery. Surrounded by the reality of the situation, his head feeling cramped by the information he'd received, Bingham was suddenly aware of the information or the timings he had not checked.

There were only two times of which he was reasonably sure: Raymond Dowdall had mentioned 12 noon as the time he'd finished his lunch and Mr Roberts had mentioned 1 o'clock as the time when a client was due to arrive. A man as fastidious as Mr Roberts, and aware as he was of Raymond's shortcomings, would have been ready for his client by 12.45. It was reasonable to suppose, then, that he'd have expected Raymond back at work by 12.30 in order to give him time to brief the lad. So, Raymond's lunch hour (and it would have been an hour!) must have run from 11.30. He would have reached the Catholic churchyard in time to finish eating his lunch by noon. It was then that he noticed two things: a man passing through the churchyard, he supposed to the river, and Janet Bawley making her way to the copse. Raymond then looked inside the church. He wouldn't have allowed more than fifteen minutes for this visit in order to give him time to get back to work. When he returned to the wall and took a second look over into the vale, Janet Bawley had already been attacked. Fifteen minutes! Raymond then went down to the river path, using the track, New Road and the lane to Bingham's right, during which time any activity by the river was hidden from him. He mentioned passing no one on the way, but on his return saw Walter Higgins by his white van. When he and Mr Roberts eventually arrived back at the junction – a period that could not have exceeded twenty minutes, even allowing for Raymond's no doubt detailed explanation – the van was no longer there.

Having thought through the sequence, Bingham was a little less annoyed with himself: the timing of each event was more important than the times themselves. But he'd failed to ask what clothes the man in the churchyard was wearing. Was he the man in the orange T-shirt? It seemed unlikely. Why would he arrive in town on an early bus for a midday meeting? Even if he wasn't the same man, what was his business at the river?

Where role, if any, did Walter Higgins play, and where was his van parked? There was no obvious place where he could avoid an obstruction. Was he one of those people who simply parked where they stopped their vehicle?

And where did Maureen Dawkins's information fit the picture? Who were the couple she claimed to see kissing and cuddling on the river path? And when was that supposed to happen? She'd been a teenager at the time. Was she alone? Was it during the school lunch hour? Was it even the same day?

It was a narrow lane but easily accessible by a vehicle. Shrouded by trees, overhung by their branches and hemmed in by ferns and ivy, it seemed to Bingham to be a gloomy but fecund place. Stinging nettles were now rife on the left-hand bank, their white blossoms still dripping with the previous night's rain; the ivy and ferns grew abundantly and gave ground cover everywhere. And then the lane opened to the sky, and there was farmland to his left, sloping down to the Churnet and stiles and farmyard gates that had been rooted in grass for years, and the trees thinned so that the remaining beeches became the copse where Janet Bawley had been murdered.

The sky was blue beyond and through the trees, and the lovers' lane became a ramblers' footpath. The copse seemed different in the morning sun, no less suggestive of a lovers' rendezvous but earthier; perhaps it was the death-cap toadstools he'd not noticed in the late afternoon light, perhaps it was his changing view of what might have happened here and subsequently.

Bingham was aware of tiredness creeping upon him. It was partly his age; he knew that to be true. He understood at seventy-five why old people sometimes seemed weary to the point of cynicism; many had given up on the belief that human nature might change for the better and that was especially difficult for someone like Bingham who'd been idealistic as a young man.

Shaking off this jaundiced feeling, he took another look around the copse where fate had struck another blow at decency, and then walked slowly back to the junction. It wasn't yet lunchtime, but he was tired and needed to sit down, preferably in a warm place. The Upton Bridge Hotel or The Tolbooth (why were two pubs so close together, he wondered) beckoned, but were they open? No! He might have guessed! But there was plenty of room to sit outside: a settle against the front wall, several open, thatched seating areas that resembled thatched huts, undercover and dry.

He smoked very occasionally – a pipe now and then, a cigar with his ex-policeman friend, Simon Brockie, or his eldest son, Paul, at Christmas – but he never carried the means with him and regretted it at that moment: he fancied drawing on a pipe, striking the match over the bowl.

There was movement in the pub. Back in Northfield he might have tapped on the window, but not here: the people didn't know him. He felt in his pocket and his hand rested on his mobile phone, a BlackBerry Lina had insisted on buying him when he'd declined her offer of what she called an iPhone. The BlackBerry was excellent: with it they'd called home from both Europe and America. He thought of his son, Ben, and he switched on the phone. Several messages were waiting on voicemail, but he ignored those and selected Ben's number.

"Dad?"

"Yes."

"I've been trying to reach you all morning."

"You've turned up something?"

"Yes. Where are you?"

Bingham gave his son directions before asking the same question.

"In a little village called Denstone. It's about a couple of miles from Upton. I'll be with you by opening time. Have a pint ready."

Bingham had a local stout, as well as a bowl of fresh water for Mollie, when Ben found him sitting in a corner table where his back could be against a wall and they settled for lunch: fried goats' cheese coated in a mixed nut crumb with mixed leaves, roasted red pepper and tomato coulis for Ben and soup of the day served with warm, crusty bread for Bingham, who had an aversion to goats' cheese, which was the only vegetarian option on the lunch menu. It was food, served hot and with pleasure by the young waitress and neither father nor son spoke until they both sat with their second pint and Mollie had spread herself across Bingham's feet.

"I've found the youth," said Ben.

Bingham, sensing his son's excitement, made no comment, but smiled and waited.

"I did as you suggested and had a chat with the barmaid. She doesn't work there in the mornings but one of the ladies who do the breakfasts rang her up for me. She didn't like to give me the girl's number, she said, 'in case, you know what'. I laughed and so did she.

Anyway, the girl spoke to me on the phone. She was embarrassed and 'what did I mean by implying' – you know the line. She was obviously surprised and worried that we'd connected her with the youth. I didn't tell her it was only a guess. Eventually – to cut a long story short – I gave her the idea that you'd bumped into the youth last night and that he'd been helpful, and you wanted to clear up one or two things he'd said. She made me promise not to get her involved and then told me that he worked for a business in Upton.

They have their premises on the High Street and specialise in laying floors, any kind of flooring: wood, bricks, vinyl, laminate, marble, ceramic, stone, concrete ... Shall I go on, Dad?"

"There's no need unless you're going into that line of business."

"I explained that friends of mine who had just moved to the district were looking for a firm with a good reputation to do some work for them and that they'd heard this firm were the tops, that a neighbour had mentioned a young man who'd done work for them and could I have a word with him. The receptionist got a bit bristly, explaining that 'Martin Newham was just one of our employees' and that 'the firm is owned by Mr Baylis, who is unavailable this morning as he is visiting customers and assessing their requirements'. I asked if I might speak with Martin Newham and was informed that he was 'on a job for Mr Baylis and would be unavailable all day'. Is it always this difficult getting information, Dad?"

"Yes, even when people are willing to talk to you. Patience and the ability to listen without interrupting are essential. Always, always you wait for that little snippet of knowledge that leads you on, opens the door … and so on. Go on."

"Well, eventually she did soften up and told me that Martin Newham was working in Denstone and 'if you are lucky you might catch him in his lunch hour'. She was a nice lady, really: just protective of her boss.

I found Martin Newham easily enough – one of Baylis's vans was parked outside the house where he was working – and I wasted no time in getting his attention. He was obstructive, at first, denying he'd ever spoken to you but when I rolled out what you'd said about him last night and Mollie had growled at him, he capitulated. I didn't threaten him with the police, but he saw me as a threat; there's no doubt about the fact.

He's a good worker – a craftsman. I saw some of the flooring he'd been laying that morning, and it was a good job. You know where the handyman types fill in the gaps round the door jambs with grouting? Not Martin: he'd cut the tiles to fit exactly the spaces they were meant to fit. I'm only pointing this out because he doesn't fit the 'keep your fucking nose out of our business' image."

"Well spotted, Ben. Go on."

"He said he just wanted to warn you for your own good because there were people in Upton who were fed up with outsiders constantly raising the Dowdall issue: the kid had been tried in a court of law and convicted, and that should be good enough. He could see there being trouble if we persisted. I asked him what sort of trouble and he was reluctant to say anything until I pressed him, when he told me that some newspaper man had been run off the road and into a field when he tried to investigate. He said: 'the bloke could have been killed'. I asked him if he meant deliberately, and he said: 'what do you think?'."

"Did you make anything of what he said?"

"He struck me as speaking the truth."

"Even if that's the case, what was his motive for doing so?"

"You don't believe it was for our own good?"

"It might have been, but it might equally have been for the good of others. How did he strike you as a person?"

"Well, there's clearly a loutishness about him but if he did speak out for our own good, I have to say that not everyone would have taken the trouble … or the risk."

"No, you're right."

"I can see that he knows more than he's saying. A bit more pressure, now that we've found him?"

"You've done well, Ben. Your morning's work has moved us on a good deal."

"And yours, Dad?"

Bingham relayed, somewhat more succinctly than his son, what had transpired at the hairdressers and the estate agents, and then relayed his thoughts

"What now?" asked Ben, running a hand through his thick, wavy hair and easing his six-foot frame back into the settle.

"I'd like to make contact with the local police ..."

"Why?"

"Did we agree ..."

"... not to interrupt one ..."

"... another? I think we did," said Bingham.

"Sorry."

"Good. I'm not sure why, to answer your question. I just know that sooner or later we're going to become involved."

"You think ..."

"I don't think anything. Sorry. I trust the British bobby. I've met too many decent ones not to do so; but I've been thinking back to the gossip in the hairdresser's this morning and I'd like to clear my head, which brings me to what I'd like you to do.

The girl mentioned – Mrs Dawkins' daughter, Maureen, – said that she'd seen a couple kissing and cuddling on the river path that morning. Given the narrow space of time – about fifteen minutes – between Raymond Dowdall claiming to have seen Janet Bawley walking to the copse and then finding her injured, we need to know exactly who she did see. *If* Janet Bawley was one of the couple, the girl must, surely, have seen her killer.

Maureen may be married and may have moved from the village, but her mother still lives here, and so take her as your starting point."

"If this Maureen lives away, I'll not be able to drive to her today."

"Why?"

"Two pints of stout."

"Four units, possibly five – one hour for each to clear the system. You can drive with two units in your blood. It's one, now: you'll be safe to drive at 4 o'clock."

"No, Dad – your generation might feel safe to drive at 4 o'clock; mine possesses a higher level of responsibility. I won't be driving until after six this evening," riposted Ben, smiling.

Father and son, leaving Ben's car at the Upton Bridge Hotel, walked slowly back into the centre of the village: Ben to, hopefully, contact Mrs Dawkins through the hairdressing salon and Bingham to return with Mollie to The White Hart, where he hoped to take a cat nap before asking where he might find the nearest police station.

After a brief enquiry at the post office on Dray Bank, Bingham returned to the pub to find a police car waiting for him.

Leaning casually against one wing of the car, a brilliant smile lighting up her brown face was a policewoman so beautiful that Bingham thought, momentarily, he might be intruding on a film set.

He'd had little to do with women officers during his time teaching; in those days, the Schools Police Liaison Officer had been a man of the old-fashioned stamp who once made the mistake of describing female officers as 'making the station look attractive', implying that was the reason for them being there in the first place. The older woman on the staff had laughed and forgiven him, and even the feminists excused the comment as 'rising from his ignorance', but the comment had stuck in Bingham's mind: it was the kind of remark, if made ten years later, that might have cost the man his job.

"You should have your dog on a lead, Mr Bingham: she could cause an accident."

"Yes, of course, you're right. My wife would agree with you whole-heartedly. Mollie is a bit of an exception but that's no excuse, I know. You're from Dudley, aren't you?"

"Bangladesh, actually," replied the officer, her lovely smile broadening into a hearty laugh, the kind that only Midland women seemed to possess. Bingham hadn't noticed anything similar in Suffolk. "I'm PC Mehreen Choudhury. I'm pleased to meet you, Mr Bingham."

"I'm originally from Wolverhampton, and that's why I recognised the accent. You are from Dudley, aren't you? I've sometimes got that mixed up with West Brom, but not often," replied Bingham, knowing a bond had been established between them so immediately he could scarce believe it. Bingham extended his hand and received a firm grip in response.

"Most people begin the other way around," replied Mehreen, "It's usually 'You're from India, aren't you, if they ask at all these days."

"It's a shame, isn't it? What's so offensive about being curious regarding a person's ethnic roots?"

"My parents came over a few years ago," replied the officer, ignoring Bingham's comment, "My father's a lawyer but I wanted a more active career. Anyway, I'm not academic by nature."

"You're certainly speedy. I've only just enquired at the post office where the nearest police station might be."

"If not 'on the spot' certainly 'on the ball', Mr Bingham."

"And a happy coincidence – that I wanted to speak with you, and you must already have wanted to speak with me."

"Yes, the local station was closed down years ago. Your nearest is now Longton – about half-an-hour away. We're Staffordshire Moorlands and your area is Waterhouses Rural. I'm a member of your NPT ..."

"Go on," urged Bingham, noting the deliberate pause and that broadening smile.

"Neighbourhood Policing Team! Not quite as immediate as your local copper on his own patch, is it? But we do our best, and I like to think a good job. I do know Upton quite well."

"Was it one of the locals told you I was here?"

"No. Let me keep my 'informer' to myself for the moment, Mr Bingham ..."

"George."

"Very well – Mehreen. We heard you were making enquiries about the murder of Janet Bawley and ...Shall we go inside? It looks like rain."

It did: the quiet, fluffy, layered clouds of the morning had begun to darken into the large, rounded masses, waves and lines that threatened rain and gusty winds, if not thunder and storm, light at first, no doubt, but increasing in ferocity. The day, early afternoon as it was, had begun to feel chilly.

In the bar over a pot of tea, Bingham sat quietly, obliging PC Choudhury to further their conversation.

"George, we know your reputation. You've been involved with the force before, haven't you, and on our side – so to speak.

Raymond Dowdall's conviction has left a bad taste in the town and each time someone tries to re-examine what happened that bad taste returns. You may have heard, already, that a journalist looking into the case was run off the road. It was a close thing: he could have been killed. The Dowdall's hired a private detective and he, too, gave up after a short time.

Sooner or later, the press gets involved and their story is always the same. They're on the side of the victim – that's how they view Mr Dowdall – and there's always a suggestion that police corruption was involved. It's taken the force a long time to try to live this down, and I doubt if we ever will, to be honest."

The speech had been rehearsed following a briefing, thought Bingham, and not very well: neither the briefing nor the speech. He had liked Mehreen Choudhury instantly and felt sorry for her: here was a decent woman doing a worthwhile job carrying out a task for what she obviously considered a doubtful reason. He said nothing.

"I've been asked to find out who requested your help in the matter?"

"It was my son. A university friend, Mervyn Ward, was at school with Raymond Dowdall."

"You've not been hired professionally?"

"Despite what the force may think, I'm not a detective, Mehreen. I think I remember being paid for two of the investigations I've carried out, but that was almost by accident."

"We know you're discreet, George, and we'd like to offer our help. If you need any of the documents regarding the case, we'd be pleased to provide them."

"But you'd like the press kept out of the matter?"

"Yes," replied Mehreen Choudhury, with a smile that linked their understanding at once. "How far have you progressed?"

Bingham related all he knew.

"You say the youth, Martin Newham, threatened you?"

"Leave it, Mehreen. He seems to be a decent lad and he's holding down a skilled job. We need people like him in this country, and he's done no harm."

"As yet. Be careful, George. I'm surprised the Dowdalls have the clothes their son was wearing at the scene of the crime. Are you sure they're genuine?"

"I've no reason to suppose otherwise. Have you met the Dowdalls?"

"No. It's like an open wound we try to keep closed … You've not yet managed to speak with Lauren Hagley or Maureen Dawkins, as was?" continued Mehreen Choudhury, referring to the notes she'd made while Bingham relayed his investigation.

"Not yet. Why do you ask about those two ladies in particular?"

"Maureen was involved with one of the appeals, as you said, and I think it might be time well spent if we take a look at what Lauren Hagley had to say at the time – if anything."

"Do I get the impression you're reopening the case?"

"No, but I might take a look at the record of the original investigation," replied PC Choudhury, standing hurriedly, "As I say, George, if we can be of any help, you have only to ask."

She extended her hand and Bingham rose to accept her handshake. He still liked the young police officer, despite harbouring the uncharitable thought that she might be trailing him.

Chapter Five

WITHOUT ANY SIGN OF ANGER

Bingham walked with the police officer to her car (although he was aware that she found his action strange) and waved his hand in a final gesture of courtesy as she drove off. For a moment – but only for a moment – he felt odd watching her car pull away; it was now the stance of the world not to bid a guest farewell: even his older son did not hang about on the porch, despite his upbringing and the attitude of both Bingham and Lina.

She was a guest, after all, because for Bingham and Ben the White Hart was home for – for how long? Bingham was unsure – and tired. He slipped back into the corner seat, cleared now of the tea service, and dozed, wondering, as he slipped into sleep, whether Ben had been successful in finding Maureen Dawkins.

Ben possessed both his father's persistence and quietude of manner; neither had ever, within their family circle, seemed capable of irritability or a sudden outburst of annoyance. Lina had always looked upon her youngest son as a cornerstone of repose: the girls, Cecilia and Fiorenza, were both capable of peevishness and Paul indulged in irascibility at times, but never her husband or Ben.

It was this quality even more than his softly spoken request that gained him a telephone call to Mrs Dawkins and a welcome to her home: the ladies of the salon had not hesitated in offering their help.

The Dawkins's house was one of many similar that bordered the road out of the town; they possessed no garages and so the residents had given their front gardens over to a parking space where cars might be kept clear of other traffic. There was no car on the Dawkins's garden, but a brick-weave spot, clearly used judging by the oil marks, was set aside for one just inside the wrought-iron gate; from this, Ben supposed that Mr Dawkins was out. A park bench overlooked a small pond in which goldfish swam surrounded by a well-kept lawn.

Mrs Dawkins had the front door open before Ben had navigated his way between an array of pot plants that lined a ruthlessly weeded footpath. She was a heavy-set woman in her fifties with a friendly smile and, judging by the neatness of her lounge, time on her hands.

"Come in, Mr Bingham, and be quick. It's chilly today but we've got the fire on. They've all left home, now – the girls, that is. There's just me and Dad."

Ben sat where he was ordered, next to the coal fire, wondering whether Mr Dawkins was the 'Dad of Dads' or just another father like his own; but he soon had a cup of tea in his hand.

"It's our Maureen you've come about, isn't it? I saw your dad today in the hairdressers. Friday's my day, but I didn't expect to see him there. You are like him to look at: taller, perhaps, but you've got the same kind eyes.

I knew he was interested even though he didn't say much. He got us women talking and that's all he wanted, I suppose. Did he find out what he needed to know? I expect so. He looks a clever man: the quiet sort but ..."

Ben didn't like to interrupt but eventually Mrs Dawkins paused, mid-sentence, and looked at him appealingly.

"... You mustn't let me go on ..."

"Dad was interested in what your daughter, Maureen, had to say."

"Maureen doesn't live here now. She's married, of course, with her own children and they live in Lichfield. Mind you, we all had to move away at the time."

Ben smiled to himself at the 'of course', spoken as though it was in the natural run of life and to be expected without question. What else would a girl do but marry?

"It was awful," continued Mrs Dawkins, "We had to leave Upton, you know. We went to live in Stoke but it was too big for me. Nice though it is, I couldn't settle there. Then we ended up in Derbyshire, on the border, in a nice little town called Bakewell, but I've always been a Staffordshire girl, and so we came back here to Upton.

Dad had had enough. We believed our lives to be in danger, see, after Maureen had given evidence at that Court of Appeal. We received anonymous threats for two years or more after that; but worse than anything, no one believed us – well, our neighbours did, of course, but no one else. It was awful, especially for the children at school. Maureen is our eldest and the others were only little then. They got picked on dreadful."

"Can you remember what happened that day?" asked Ben, trying desperately to focus on the events of the time.

"On the day poor Janet Bawley was murdered you mean?"

"Yes."

"The children were home in the lunch hour. I always had them home for lunch: you know what they're eating then. They were playing on their bikes where we park the car. Dad was at work, see. Well, I set off to get them back to school for a quarter past one and I was in the High Street when I saw the police car rushing down New Road. There were several mothers standing around and they said they'd seen John Boardman, he's our local man – or was fourteen years ago – going down to the river. One of them – Mrs Shreeve, I believe – said she'd taken her children back early that day because she was catching the bus into Stoke and when she got to the corner of the High Street and New Road she saw young Raymond Dowdall running hell for leather to Mr Roberts office …"

Ben listened, wondering, as his father had done many times, how police officers sorted the salient from the irrelevant. Not, in a sense, that any of what Mrs Dawkins said was irrelevant: it did confirm the timings given by Raymond and Mr Roberts.

"… covered with blood, he was, she said. All over his trousers and hands. Raymond, that is: not Mr Roberts. When Mr Roberts came out, he looked white with worry and hurried on down to the river with the lad. I waited a bit and eventually the ambulance came, and someone said that Janet Bawley had been attacked and it was a matter of life and death."

"Did Mrs Shreeve or anyone who saw Raymond running up the hill tell the police what they'd seen?"

"Oh yes. Mrs Shreeve said the police – John Boardman, that is – came around the same night but her little boy was in bed and John didn't like to wake him – he's a light sleeper – and so he'd come round the next day and talk to her. But he never did."

"They never took a statement?"

"No, not from Mrs Shreeve or anyone on the New Road or at the Upton Bridge, which is just across the way from where it happened."

"So, where was Maureen while this was going on?" asked Ben, eager to pin down the fifteen-year old's movements.

"She'd been off school for a few days with a very bad cold. Maureen never really took to school. Any excuse, but she was poorly that day, and she'd taken our dog for a walk. That's how she came to be down by the river."

"Was she alone?"

"She never said. I think so. Is that important, Mr Bingham?"

"It might be. What did she say when she got home?"

"Nothing much. She said she'd found Scamp along the riverside path, where he liked to go when he escaped from the garden, and then she came home."

"She never mentioned the couple she later claimed to see kissing and cuddling?"

"Not at the time. It was later she thought of them."

"And she never mentioned seeing a man with a white van?"

"No."

Ben felt tired. Culling useful information from Mrs Dawkins was like drawing blood from the proverbial stone. He decided to try one last tack.

"So, it was only after Maureen gave evidence at the appeal that your family received these threats? There were none at the time?"

"There wouldn't be, would there?"

There might have been, thought Ben, if the man had seen Maureen on the day; there might have been if Maureen had been meeting someone else down by the river. As his father had said, it was all so tight a timetable.

"I was walking back home down the High Street one night when a car pulled up beside me," continued Mrs Dawkins, "They wound down the window and said 'You and your daughter had better keep your mouths shut or it will be the worse for you and your kids'. I believe that was after the trial but before the appeal, now you mention it.

And Dad – he works at the local quarry – said that one of his workmates, two or three years after the murder, said to him 'It's a shame that Raymond Dowdall's doing time for someone else. I know who did it'."

Ben suddenly felt refreshed. He remembered his father saying after the Beddoes case 'someone, somewhere knows something, whether they are aware of the fact or not and over time loyalties change, memories slip out of control and guilt digs in'. Not that he thought Mrs Dawkins had any reason to feel guilt, but her memory had certainly slipped, and he was in possession of two memories unearthed by their conversation.

"Thank you, Mrs Dawkins, that's most helpful."

"It was a terrible time. You just want to forget it."

"Yes, of course. It might be helpful if I could speak with your husband."

"I don't know about that. Reg just wants to forget it. We never talk about it in the house. He says things have settled down. Let them rest."

"Perhaps your daughter, Maureen, might talk to me?"

"Maureen's another matter. She's twenty-nine now, you know. She was that afraid after the appeal, she went abroad for a while and worked in one of them holiday resorts. She thought they were out to get her."

Ben didn't ask who 'they' might be. He didn't want to interrupt the flow of Mrs Dawkins's concerns.

"I think she might talk to you, but not here. I'll give her a ring when you've gone and ask her. She'll be at work now, but she's home this evening. I don't know whether her husband will mind, mind. He's been a brick, he has. If it weren't for him, I don't think Maureen would have come back home."

"They met abroad, did they?"

"He was on holiday at the resort where she worked. They fell in love and it was David that persuaded her to come home. They've got two children now and live in Lichfield ... Oh there, I've told you ..."

"You've told me nothing, Mrs Dawkins, that you need worry about. If Maureen doesn't want to talk to us, then the matter's closed. If she does, we'll go to her house. My dad knows Lichfield. He grew up in Wolverhampton and Lichfield was one of the places he talked about when we were children. I believe his parents had friends there. He always spoke of it as a nice place."

Ben wasn't sure why he found himself rattling on about Lichfield but it seemed to soothe Mrs Dawkins and so he put his ramblings down to instinct. 'Never mind the manuals,' his father had once said, 'The best kind of management is instinct'.

"She might see you. Our Maureen was angry at the time."

And her anger invoked courage because the phone call came as Ben and his father were enjoying their second dinner at the White Hart: Bingham a green curry and Ben a ginger root stir-fry with vegetables, chilli and onion. Neither drank a drop but promised each other a session when they returned from Lichfield.

During the drive, Bingham talked about the attractions of the town: Samuel Johnson's birthplace, Erasmus Darwin's house, the National Memorial Arboretum, the cathedral and the Garrick Theatre. Ben listened without hearing because Bingham had told him to watch out for the road to ensure they were not followed from Upton. The precaution seemed to verge on paranoia but the experiences of the Dawkins family and the fact that Bingham himself had been given a 'warning' suggested the need to be wary, and he had no wish to bring violence into the life of the young woman who had agreed to talk to them.

North of Uttoxeter, Ben turned east taking the rote through Doveridge and Sudbury and then south through Yoxall. Twice he pulled over and waited before continuing. South of Yoxall, he turned east through

Orgreave and so past the arboretum his father had spoken about. It was over an hour before they entered Lichfield.

Maureen's husband, David, opened the door to the Binghams, a frown across his forehead, a guarded smile on his lips.

"Come in and welcome," he said, shutting the door quickly behind them, "You understand the conditions, don't you – nothing of what Maureen's to say must get back to who it might concern as coming from her."

"Do you mind if we bring Mollie in?" asked Bingham, "She frets if left alone."

"No, of course not. Sit yourselves down and Maureen'll be with you in a minute. She's just putting the children to bed and then she'll be down. Can I get you anything?"

"A cup of tea would be welcome, Mr Bridge. Thank you," replied Bingham.

David Bridge was pouring the tea as his wife arrived. Bingham had been picturing Maureen Dawkins, now Bridge, ever since a meeting seemed likely, and she was all he anticipated. She was taller than her mother but with the same fresh, open face. Her skin shone with health and honesty. Maureen was the kind of person Bingham had learned to trust and she would be a supportive colleague in any job: the kind of person who said to your face what she might say behind your back – or, there again, might not say. She was no gossip and no doubt scorned those who indulged in chitchat. She was much slimmer than he'd imagined; her figure was one that would be described as desirable. She possessed a gentleness of manner that appealed to him. He saw her tucking her children into bed and sensed the feeling of contentment as she did so. Bingham noticed a look pass between her and her husband: a smile, shared understanding. Bingham stood and thanked her for seeing them.

"I could do no less, Mr Bingham. I was surprised the judge refused to accept my evidence at the time of Mr Dowdall's appeal. Oh, the dog! It's a pity the children are in bed. They'll be annoyed at not seeing her. How can I help best?"

"Start at the beginning, if you would, and just talk us through. If I could make notes of any questions that arise, I'd be grateful. I can then ask them without interrupting you," Bingham replied, adding when he noticed the husband's concern, "I'll not write down anything you say, and you can tear up the questions when we've finished."

"That will put David's mind at rest," replied Maureen Bridge with a smile, and looked up at her husband before continuing, "I was out looking for Scamp. I knew where he might be and so I followed the walks we usually took down to the Churnet. I'd gone all the way along the river path and seen no one. This would have been before twelve o'clock because I found Scamp a long way off down by a spot where he liked to get into the river. I stayed with him for a while and then we made our way back. I wasn't feeling very well, and so I didn't want to stay too long, much as he loved the river. It was so quiet. I was surprised when I got near the end of the path to see this couple. They were – you know. And it was broad daylight.

I didn't know who it was at the time, but then I saw her photograph in the newspapers and realised I'd seen Janet Bawley with this man. I didn't know who he was either, but he was a stocky person with broad shoulders and had thick hair – not long but thick – and he was wearing a corduroy jacket and jeans and his boots – they were workman's boots and dirty – yes, light brown and covered in dirt. I didn't want to attract their attention and so I put Scamp on the lead and hurried away. I went back up New Road and through the village home.

I suppose you're wondering why I didn't come forward at the time. Well, I was afraid the man might have seen me hurry away with Scamp. When I read what had happened to Mrs Bawley, I didn't want the same thing to happen to me. I was only fifteen, you know – just a child, really ... and then I saw the article in the newspaper and realised that Raymond had been found guilty of the murder. I knew he couldn't have done it. We were at school together, although he was two years ahead of me. I did know him because we both came from Upton.

The article talked about Raymond using his lunchtime as an alibi to hide his intentions, but I knew that was silly. Raymond wasn't capable of thinking that way. He'd told the truth at his trial and I was the only one who knew that was so.

I didn't go to the police straight away because the police seemed so confident. Everyone thought they'd got the right person. I thought, perhaps, that Raymond had attacked Mrs Bawley later in the afternoon, but it kept playing on my mind and then I learned that Mrs Bawley had been killed soon after I saw her. And I was terrified. I realised I'd seen her killer.

I still didn't know what to do. After all, the man was still out there somewhere. Eventually, I told Mum what

I'd seen, and she told Dad and he said that I should go to the police and 'make a clean breast of it'. They were his exact words, but I knew what he meant and so I went to see John Boardman and he referred me to his HQ. He took me, along with Dad, and they listened to what I had to say, and I think they believed me but said I must have got the wrong day. I knew it wasn't the wrong day because I'd been off with a cold and I remembered that well enough, and so did Mum."

Living the memory again, fourteen years on, brought back the fear of the time. The fresh-faced young woman became the frightened schoolgirl, and her husband sat down beside Maureen on the sofa and enfolded her in his arms.

"I think that's enough now," he said, but without any sign of anger.

"No, David, I must go on. Otherwise, there's no point … After the appeal hearing, where I gave my evidence, I received threats and so did my family. Whoever the man was with Mrs Bawley, he must have read in the newspapers about me giving evidence. Nasty threats they were. I was told to keep my mouth shut or I'd end up like Mrs Bawley," continued Maureen, her lips trembling, "I was told there was a contract out on me and if I opened my mouth again I'd be shot. That was when we moved away from Upton and, eventually, I went abroad. I was only just seventeen when I went but they were kind to me at the resort and I learned to forget about what had happened. I don't think there's any more I can tell you, Mr Bingham, unless you've any questions."

"Just a few, if I may," said Bingham, quietly, "Firstly, what time was it you saw this man with Mrs Bawley?

This is quite critical, and so if you can't remember don't guess."

"I was sure of the time, Mr Bingham. I heard the church clock strike twelve as Scamp and I were walking along the river path. So, it must have been a few minutes after."

"The boots. You said they were dirty. What colour was the dirt?"

"Blackish, but it may have looked like that because it was on a light brown boot."

"And you heard no voices at all – no shouts, no cries?"

"Nothing."

"Not even when you were walking away up New Road?"

"No."

"And you saw no one, no vehicle or anything else on the road?"

"No."

"I know you didn't see the man's face, but would you recognise him again if you saw him?"

"Yes, I would."

"But you never have?"

"No. David and I have never been back to Upton. Mum and Dad always visit us here."

"Mrs Bridge, we cannot thank you enough for your help. Rest assured that nothing of what you've said will come back to you. Enjoy your life, your husband and your family with peace of mind."

"Have I been of help, Mr Bingham. It seems awful that Raymond Dowdall has been in prison all these years for a crime he did not commit. If what I've said has been useful, I'll be eternally grateful if it secures his release. I know you'll be discreet and do nothing to bring this down on our heads; but if you need me again, I am willing to help."

"I know that's so, Mrs Bridge. Everything about you tells me it is so, but we'll keep you and your loved ones out of this business. Have no fear."

Bingham and his son were back at the White Hart before either of them spoke again; the bar had cleared of drinkers; the barman had switched off the lights and the pumps and left the two of them with a final beer before saying a cheerful 'goodnight'.

"Even if the police believed the lady had got the days mixed up, I would have thought they might have tried to track down the man she saw. If Mrs Bawley was with a man, a man she knew well enough to be putting her arms around, he must surely have been of interest," said Ben.

"My thoughts exactly," replied Bingham, pleased that he and his son were that much alike and of a single mind.

Chapter Six

LISTENING PATIENTLY, WITHOUT INTERRUPTING

When Bingham got to his room, he found the note shoved under the door; it informed him that a lady had telephone the White Hart at 7 o'clock and left her number. He knew immediately who the lady must be.

The following morning, he set out early, as the note suggested he talked with her before she left for work: 'otherwise, Mr Bingham, we may have to wait until this evening as Saturday is a busy day at the salon'. The advice suited Bingham: he was always up at six o'clock and walking the four dogs soon after, having taken Lina a cup of tea in bed.

With Mollie at his side, he set off along the High Street. He turned into New Road and then veered off to his left along Coopers Way, a narrow road, almost a lane, crowded with a mixture of houses and bungalows, all unique, all different except for their stone-laid walls and immaculately coiffured privet hedges. Lina cared for their garden and with her Italianate terrace in mind would have admired the neatness of the hedging, although for the most part their farmhouse, deep in the Suffolk countryside, appeared to have grown out of the environment rather than having been imposed upon it, surrounded as it was by fields.

He came to a chalet bungalow on his right, set back from the road and fronted by a stone paved driveway. The privet hedge was short compared with the others he'd seen and set upon a stone wall whose blocks were cemented together. The driveway was clear: no car, no pots of plants, no clutter of any kind. On the front of the bungalow a tall window allowed light onto a small lobby. To the right of this, Bingham noticed a bedroom and further along a single garage with an up-and-over door. As he turned to walk towards the front door, Mollie held back.

"What's up? Oh, of course. Sorry. Let's find some grass."

They didn't have to go far: where their road met Horse Road, opposite the salon, a telegraph pole rose from a small stretch of manicured grass and it was here that Mollie was able to relieve herself. She was fastidious in her ablutions, insisting upon grass as opposed to a hard surface and had never fouled a footpath in her life. Bingham did the necessary with a black bag and they made their way back to the bungalow. Lauren Hagley was waiting at the front door.

"I saw you pass, Mr Bingham. I thought you'd missed me," and continued, "Oh, give it to me, I'll deal with it," once Bingham had explained.

Bingham could have described the front room before Lauren Hagley invited him to sit down. The driveway had said everything; there was nothing out of place. He might have walked into a show house on a new estate: a wooden floor set off a cream three-piece suite on which the cushions were puffed to perfection. On a central coffee table was bowl of fruit, all fresh and with the apples polished. There wasn't a blemish on the furniture or a speck of dust on the floor. He looked at Mollie and Lauren Hagley read his thoughts.

"She's fine, Mr Bingham. I'm pleased you've managed to get here early. I thought you might and so I had my breakfast as soon as I got up but would you like a cup of tea. I'm having another one."

Bingham had only glimpsed Lauren Hagley the previous morning when she arrived at work; the image he retained of her suggested one word: smart. She was a very slim woman, her slimness the type a woman he'd known as a young man told him indicated sexiness: 'slim women are sexier because their nerve ends are nearer the surface', she'd explained. Bingham hadn't argued.

Lauren Hagley was certainly attractive and neatly dressed in a style all her own. She reminded Bingham of the 1950s but not in an old-fashioned way; her clothes were all modern and yet placed with a precision not noticeable today. She sat opposite Bingham and leaned slightly towards him, her legs together and slanted to one side.

A woman in her mid-forties, thought Bingham, a prime time for many; with the child-bearing years out of the way, there came a kind of freedom denied a younger woman. And there was perceptiveness in the way she looked at him, as though she read his thoughts without too much trouble.

"I'm pleased you could come, Mr Bingham. There are things I need to clear up. Janet and I were friends. We were at school together and we went after our first boyfriends together. You understand?"

The question indicated a certain reluctance to go on if Bingham did not appreciate what Lauren Hagley was telling him; a confidence was coming, and she wanted to know that he was sympathetic. He nodded and smiled.

"I think you may have heard rumours about Janet, and I don't want you to get the wrong idea about her. You need to understand the kind of person she was before you pass judgement."

It was Bingham's way to sit listening patiently, without interrupting but he felt Lauren Hagley needed reassurance.

"I'm not in the habit of judging people, Mrs Hagley ..."

"Lauren, please."

"Very well – I'm George. As I said, I'm not in the habit of making judgements. Judgements are easy to make; it's understanding that requires the effort."

Lauren Hagley smiled: suddenly relieved, suddenly aware she could speak freely to this man.

"Oh, good. I know you've come here to help Raymond Dowdall and I think you should. I believe him to be innocent, but I don't want Janet maligned along the way. I expect you've been told that she was ... promiscuous and ... and that's true. I must say that: it's true. But she was a nice person. Everyone liked Janet. Do you understand?"

Bingham nodded and smiled again.

"In a way, I blame her husband ..."

"She was married?"

"Yes. Didn't you know?"

"No. My son and I only arrived on Thursday afternoon. Please go on, Lauren. Just tell it your way."

"Mark is a surveyor. He works in Stoke. He was always away from home from early morning and often 'til late in the evening. Janet was on her own all day, when she wasn't working.

As well as being a hairdresser she was also a makeup artist. She'd done a course at the local tech when we were teenagers and she got a lot of work on the side – you know, weddings, hen parties, functions, that kind of thing. So, she was away from home, sometimes in the evenings, sometimes at weekends. She liked the work and it supplemented what she earned at the salon. As you can imagine, in a town like Upton there's a limit to what you can earn hairdressing.

As I said, everyone liked Janet. She was easy company. She was good-natured, personable; and so, she got recommendations. They only had the one car and Mark needed that for work, and so people gave her lifts to where she was needed … She was an attractive woman, you see, and she enjoyed the attention. It was easy for her to form liaisons with men … as her circle of friends widened, she received offers …"

Lauren Hagley looked at Bingham, daring him to pass criticism of her friend; but he merely smiled and continued to listen patiently. It wasn't his world and never had been even in the days before he and Lina met, but he'd come across women like the Janet Bawley who her friend was conjuring before him. He wondered why she troubled to do so, but only briefly; somehow, he saw where her revelations were drifting.

"It was the excitement that urged her on," said Bingham, and his comment wasn't a question.

"Yes," replied Lauren Hagley, a note of relief in her voice, "She became fascinated with the risk of being caught. She looked for public places. It was a challenge to her. She thought it a huge joke …"

"Go on," suggested Bingham, aware of the woman's hesitation.

"Janet kept a little black book of what she called 'her conquests'. She rated their performance on a scale of one to five," said Lauren Hagley, unable to hide a smile.

"Was the existence of this book known generally?"

"It did cause some concern in certain circles."

"No doubt. You saw this book; Janet discussed it with you."

"Yes."

"And so, you know the names of the men concerned?" asked Bingham, and this time it was a question because it occurred to him that Janet Bawley might have used codenames.

"Yes."

"And they're the names you want to give me."

"I wrote them down in case ... in case I trusted you not to malign Janet," replied Lauren Hagley.

She went to a sideboard, where Bingham had noticed several family photographs: children at various stages with a woman who was clearly Lauren and an older woman who was equally clearly her mother. There was no man in any of the photographs. She retrieved her list from one of the drawers and handed it to Bingham; as he expected, it was neatly written in an open italic hand, one learned at school and remembered.

Bingham placed the list in his notebook, spending a few moments to compare the names with those he'd already been given by Roberta Dowdall.

"It takes two to tango," he said, "Was Janet passed around by these men?"

"They are all in business of one kind or another. Some are professional men: others are ... well, one is a hotelier, another runs a haulage firm. I've written their addresses against their names, and their work."

"So, I see. Janet moved in wealthy and influential circles. Are you sure these names are genuine? There's no chance is there ..."

"... that Janet was showing off? No, Mr Bingham, there isn't!"

"Tell me about her husband – Mark, wasn't it? It's the first I've heard of him."

"He's a nice man but consumed by his work. If only he'd spent more time with Janet none of this might have happened. They married soon after he finished university and came back here, but their marriage hit the rocks and Janet moved out for a while. She took digs. There's a stone quarry near here. She took digs in the village next door."

"Did she work there – at the quarry?"

"For a while. She took several jobs when she and Mark split up. None lasted long. They got back together, eventually. I think he really loved her but just didn't appreciate what Janet needed."

"Did they continue to live in the town?"

"No. They both wanted a fresh start and bought an old farmhouse away from the village, near Stone. Mark bought her a little car so Janet could get about and didn't feel trapped. He thought that renovating the farmhouse would give her something to do."

"She was keen on the renovation?"

"For a while. Janet was like that: her enthusiasm came in phases."

"Why did you never tell the police what you've just told me?"

"Isn't that obvious!"

"Yes, in some respects, but I'd still like to near it from you."

"I do not appreciate being bullied, Mr Bingham."

"You've sat on this information believing in the possibility that an innocent man was imprisoned for a crime he did not commit," replied Bingham, inserting a query into his tone to soften the accusation.

"There was other evidence against Raymond Dowdall."

"Yes, but knowing Janet Bawley as you did, and holding the information you possessed, it certainly occurred to you that others may have had a motive to kill your friend."

"Yes."

"And yet you said nothing."

"I want justice for Janet, but I do not want her maligned in the process."

"Others in Upton must know what you do even if they do not have the actual names. Janet's reputation must already be a source of gossip and must have been at the time."

"That's different from having it dragged through the courts, possibly unnecessarily."

Bingham wondered how often the concept of 'unnecessary' arose when it came to the question of justice. Was it ever unnecessary – perhaps inconvenient would be a better word – to arrive at the truth? While no one wanted a guilty man to go unpunished and an innocent man to be imprisoned was that the lesser of evils? After all, it could be a salve to the conscience that Raymond Dowdall was happy enough in prison – perhaps happier than someone like him might be out in the community. And what good would it do – and what harm might it engender – to seek the truth?

"I know what you're thinking, Mr Bingham, but I would ask you to bear in mind that it was me who approached you."

"Because I'm not a police officer."

"Yes. I ask for your discretion. Did you notice one name in particular on the list?"

"Yes. While not identical your list bears considerable resemblance to another given to me."

"By the Dowdalls?"

"Yes. I take it that you want your name kept out of whatever may happen?"

"I'm not a coward, George, and I'd like to see Janet's killer brought to justice."

"Have you never approached anyone else in the way you've approached me?"

"No! There was a newspaper man at the time of one of the appeals but the information I held would have been meat and gravy to a journalist."

"Thank you for your help, Lauren. I'll do what I can."

They shook hands in a friendly enough manner at the front door and Bingham made his way back to The White Hart. As he hurried along for what would be a late-than-usual breakfast, he noticed storm clouds gathering and the air had turned cold. It did not bode well but Bingham nonetheless felt a sense of relief that he and his son were not on what had been intended as a walking break.

Bingham's walk and the sudden chill in the air had sharpened his appetite and he tucked into an unusually large breakfast: two eggs scrambled rather than one and a couple of vegetarian sausages tossed alongside followed by toast and marmalade and two cups of scalding hot tea. Ben had waited for his father and enjoyed his customary Full English.

Once the table had been cleared and the ladies thanked, Ben, who had clearly been eager to tell his father something, opened up.

"I phoned Paul while you were out."

"Why?"

"Yesterday, you asked me to give him a ring regarding blood loss in anyone battered almost to death with a branch."

"Oh yes. I imagine he was pleased to help at this hour of the morning."

Ben laughed: his brother's grumpiness on waking or when tired was a byword in the family. This was probably an unfair one since he was now a GP and used to being called out at unreasonable hours; besides he had a family of his own and must, with three children, be accustomed to waking through the night.

"He was a bit tetchy," replied Ben, "and advised that you kept your nose out of murder cases, but he was helpful. He said that a violent blow or blows in the region of the head would produce a spray of blood that would appear as very tiny spots on any surface they hit, such as clothing.

I told him that the woman had sat up suddenly when Raymond turned her over and I asked him if this would account for the spots of blood on Raymond's shirt and tie. He thought that was unlikely because she would have had to shake herself about violently for that to happen. He also said that the harder the blow, the smaller the spots of blood would be."

"And so, the only way Raymond's clothes could have been splattered with blood as they were would be if he had struck the blows?"

"Yes, but Paul went on to say that we would need to know how many times the woman was struck. I told him that there was a great deal of blood on the ground where she had fallen, and he went on to say that that suggested she had been struck several times."

"A ferocious attack?"

"Yes."

"Raymond said that he took off his fleece before he knelt down to turn Janet Bawley over. If he'd attacked her, he'd hardly be cool enough to remove his fleece first, would he? And the only bloodstain on the fleece was his own footmark, made when he got up after turning her over."

"He said 'there was a lot of blood by the side of her head and her hair was soaked with it. I reached over to feel her pulse, and it was then that she sat up'. So, her heart was still pumping at that point," said Ben.

"We're out of our depth, aren't we, Ben? This surmise is little better than gossip. If science didn't solve this case at the trial, it isn't going to solve it now."

"Unless relevant forensic evidence was missing or withheld at the trial?"

"Hmm! We're coming to a rather tricky part of our investigation now and we need to be careful, Ben. You've placed our youth from Walsall and our man with the white van. I've seen Mr Roberts and we've both seen the Dowdalls. Apart from wading through their mass of paperwork – and I haven't the stomach for that this morning – I think there's little to be gained from paying them another visit at the moment. What we do have are two lists of names; it's these people we need to place at the time of Janet Bawley's killing, and none of them is obliged to be helpful."

"Especially if they've something to hide."

"Precisely, and that may be a key to the door. But do you get the impression that there may be little sympathy for Raymond Dowdall's plight in this town? If that's the case, we might be told to sod off and there's nothing we can do about it. Let's take a long look at Lauren Hagley's list – she's the lady I saw this morning – and decide where to go from there. But tread carefully, Ben, tread carefully."

When the two of them, father and son, stepped outside nearing coffee time, the rain was coming down in sheets, lashing their faces and hands, soaking them through in minutes and causing their clothes to cling to their bodies. It was a typical English autumn: one day fine and sunny, the next a family's garments would litter the house in their dampness, drying on radiators, hanging from doors.

Ben, unfortunately for him, had opted for the walk to the Ramblers' Rest, the owner's name being one on the list of Janet Bawley's alleged lovers. He was a successful hotelier, no doubt a man of substance in Staffordshire, a Chamber of Commerce man, one who would decide whether a one-way system through the town (which would benefit the pedestrians) might harm his business or those of his fellows and decide accordingly.

This, of course, was pure speculation on Ben's part: neither he nor his father had ever met the man who might be of a completely different calibre. Ben's task was to engage the staff in conversation and find out what he could, anything that could possibly be of importance.

He had dressed himself to look the part of the rambler he had intended to be and with Mollie in her raincoat at his side made his way down New Road and so to the junction that spurred off four ways: one to where Janet Bawley was murdered, another along Green Lane to the Ramblers' Rest. It was a narrow road, barely more than a metalled country lane: to one side Toothill Wood rose high on the hillside, to the other, hedges crowded in on the walkers.

The rain came down in torrents pouring mud from the hillside across the road. Mollie seemed to dance over the rushing water while Ben splashed through, a child again, remembering when he had his 'great big waterproof boots on' and enjoyed this kind of weather. Nevertheless, he was looking forward to a hot toddy at the bar.

The hedges opened up slightly as they progressed and to his left Ben saw the Churnet wending its own way along the vale. He passed a dog walker, a woman stooped under her plastic rainhat from where the precipitation splashed, little sprays of water bouncing with unexpected violence onto her shoulders and directly down to her feet. There were no cars on the road, and he was glad of the reassurance that gave: dodging them would have involved diving into the hedge and risking a roll down the embankment into the river below, never mind Mollie wandering at will, ahead or astern of him as the mood took her.

Further along, fields, rain-washed and windswept, appeared to his right and the sky opened to his gaze, black and threatening a long, wet day; and then he and his dog were enclosed again as more trees sprang from the verge, leaning into the road, dripping rain.

A small lane appeared to Ben's left and on the corner an elderly woman stood, a shopping bag clutched against her, as though waiting for a bus. The lane, Ben decided, must lead to a private house. He kept to the road, which now became narrower than ever, barely leaving room for a car and making it impossible for two to pass each other.

A Forestry Commission notice informed him that there was no overnight parking allowed on a stretch of land to this left that served as a carpark and that the place closed at six in the evening. Today, not surprisingly, the spot was empty of vehicles and functioned only as a mud-bath for a family of ducks that had made their way up from the Churnet.

And then, suddenly, he saw the sky to his left, thick with clouds, rising above the dark trees and the Ramblers Rest appeared, not so much the cosy retreat he'd imagined but more like a country club. A large notice informed him that it was open and possessed its own carpark to the rear. Shaking raindrops from his hat and nose, Ben headed for a gap in the stone wall surrounding the premises, anticipating a hot drink and an early lunch. He looked down at Mollie and was sure she smiled at what he was thinking.

Bingham, pleased his son had selected the short straw, lingered at The White Hart for a while, intending to use Ben's car for a drive out of the village to another address, this one from Roberta Dowdall's list: the home of a Gerald Osman, who lived alone, apparently in a rundown house that was part of a hamlet on the edge of the Peak District.

But his trip was not to be – at least, for that day. He was sitting over a cup of strong, black coffee when the phone rang, and he answered it.

"I understand you have a guest by the name of Bingham. Is he still in, by any chance?"

"In and answering."

"I beg your pardon."

"I'm George Bingham. I happened to be in the bar."

"Mr Bingham? That's very convenient. Is there any possibility that we might have a chat? My name's John Hayes. I'm a journalist – or I was – and I may be of some help to you."

"I'll wait here for you if you've no objection to meeting in the pub."

"No, I think that should be all right. I live in Matlock. I'll be there in about forty-five minutes."

John Hayes was a tall, distinguished-looking man in his late sixties or, possibly, early seventies. Bingham wasn't sure but took to him immediately. A pair of rimless glasses accentuated a pair of smiling eyes, a smile picked up by the man's mouth. He was smartly dressed, even to the point of wearing a tie, a fact Bingham found odd in a man who he thought must obviously be retired; since giving up work, Bingham had never worn a tie and had always worn it loosened when at work.

"Once a journalist, always a journalist?" queried Bingham, with a grin, after they'd introduced themselves.

"You're suspicious of journalists, George?"

"I must confess, I've been wondering what's in this meeting for you. I don't think a newspaperman ever turns his back on the possibility of a story."

"It's in the blood. Once we're on the scent, it's against our nature to lose the trail."

"Still," replied Bingham, "in a pack of jackals there must be at least one noble beast."

Both men laughed. A remark that could have been gratuitously offensive was not taken as such; it stemmed from a sense of humour shared by men of their generation, men who could be rude to one another without being either disagreeable or insulting. It was a question of give and take: if you could dish it out, you must be able to take it back.

"But I am here to help. I heard that you and your son were looking into the Dowdall affair. I did the same many years ago at the request of Ray's parents and I gave evidence at his appeals ... To no avail."

"You believe in his innocence?"

"I have no doubt about it, George. Do you?"

"I reserve judgement."

"You won't, after we've had a talk and you've had a chance to go through the paperwork I've gathered over the years and brought with me. But first, I want to give you a warning. You and your son are on dangerous ground. It suits many people in this town that Ray should take the blame for Janet's murder. The trail I spoke of involved intimidation and attempts to kill me."

John Hayes made his comments without dramatizing himself; his voice was calm and matter of fact, his face didn't lose the cheery smile it seemed to possess habitually.

Both men sat down, as though by mutual consent, at the table where Bingham had enjoyed his coffee: Bingham, out of habit, with his back to the wall,

John Hayes with his to the bar. He leaned forward and spoke in a soft, gentle voice.

"I'd turned out to what I understood was an accident at a local quarry. It was against my practice to go out at night if it involved isolated places, but it was a young woman who phoned, and I was the editor. It seemed genuine enough and it doesn't pay to appear uninterested and the details she gave seemed authentic.

I was up in the Staffordshire hills where the roads twist and turn. I imagine you're used to country words where you come from? Suddenly, out of nowhere, there was a huge truck behind me. Its headlights were full on; the driver made no attempt to dip and I was relieved when I found a passing place. I pulled in expecting the truck to go on by, but he didn't. He slowed. I could see the driver because his cab light was on, and he appeared to be talking to someone on his mobile phone.

I knew fear, then, George, I can tell you. I think it's the first time in my life I've actually sweated with fear. It was instinct, I suppose. I just knew the call had been a hoax and I'd been lured out into the hills. I decided to make a dash for it. The driver was a big bloke, burly, and I didn't fancy him getting out of his cab and coming for me.

I decided to drive like hell until I reached a side road and then turn sharply, hoping the truck would shoot by. There was no way that he could have done a U-turn on that road. He was right on my tail when I turned, and he careered down the hill. But I no sooner thought I'd evaded him when he appeared again. He must have reversed, and that took some nerve on those narrow roads. His cab was still lit, and he was driving one-handed because I could see that he was still on the phone. His lights blinded me and then he blared his horn and rammed my car. It jolted me forward and I felt sicker than ever. Again, the horn and another jolt. I thought I'd lose control of the car.

I knew the road. Ahead was a fork. Perhaps I could try and throw him off once more. If only I could reach a main road, I thought he would give up. But as I approached the fork, I saw a vehicle – it looked like a dumper truck – parked sideways across the road, and I knew I'd been pursued into a trap. Someone was standing by the dumper truck and he had something in his hand. I don't what it was, but I knew it bode me no good.

What on Earth could I do?"

John Hayes paused, as his story re-ignited the memory of that night. He smiled.

"My guardian angel must have been watching over me, although my ordeal was not over. To my right, I saw an open gateway. I slowed, hit the brake and swung into what I supposed would be a field. My pursuer had no chance; he shot forward and I heard an almighty crash. I knew he'd hit the dumper, but I was still in trouble. The field was muddy: it was this time of year and we'd had a lot of rain. My car was stuck. I decided to make a run for it. Fortunately, I am a hill walker and I knew my way. But for that knowledge they would have caught me, I'm sure. I heard them give chase, but I had a head start and I was off like a fox outthinking the hunt.

I had my car retrieved the next day and reported the matter to the police, but nothing came of it. Whatever damage was done to either of the trucks had either been hidden or repaired.

This was part of a pattern that emerged once I started looking into ray's case. You'll find other incidents recorded in these papers I'll leave with you."

Bingham had several questions he wanted to ask but sat quietly, waiting for John Hayes to recover his composure. It was as they sat in thought that Bingham's phone rang.

"This is the Royal Stoke University Hospital, Mr Bingham. Your son, Ben, has just been admitted to A& E. Are you able to come at once?"

Chapter Seven
STILL STRUGGLING

Bingham never quite forgave himself for his first thought when he switched off his phone following the call from the Royal Stoke: 'what had happened to Mollie?' It's true the nurse informed him that Ben's injuries were not life-threatening and that he was concerned for his son: but nevertheless! Sometime later, when he finally came around to admitting this to Lina, she only laughed and commented that Ben had told her as much.

John Hayes immediately offered to drive, "since I know Stoke and the roads", and Bingham was grateful: he still felt competent at the wheel and had no intention of relinquishing his right to drive but his mind was on his son and what might have happened to him. Besides, the rain that soaked him on his visit to Lauren Hagley had not ceased; low-lying parts of the country would soon be receiving their flood warnings.

Rain slashed at the windscreen of John Hayes's car forcing the wipers into overdrive. Where the road cambered unevenly or dipped, huge puddles had already gathered, and the car brushed sprays of water aside into the hedgerows. In places, the falling rain had closed off roads completely so that cars pressed gingerly on, sometimes waiting for another vehicle to test the depth of water first. The newspaperman leaned forward over his wheel, peering through the deluge that clung like bubble-wrap to the windscreen. Occasionally, he caught a particularly heavy flood and the car lurched to one side, leaning either into the ditch or the oncoming traffic.

Bingham had known Stoke well as a student because he'd attended Keele University but had not returned there much since that time and not at all since the death of his mother in 2006. Peering through the curtains of rain that swished around them like a pallid version of the Northern Lights, he was amazed at how the city, like so many others, had changed since his student days, carved up as it was by new road systems. No longer, it seemed, was it possible to amble the streets as he once had done. Were there still, somewhere, the little pockets of community he had come to know so well? He'd liked Stoke and its people: amiable, quiet, welcoming and with a gentle sense of humour.

And then, through the sheets of rain he saw the Royal Stoke: modern-looking, no doubt purposeful, a dream of a design, well-signposted. Times move on. John Hayes dropped him at the front entrance and pulled off to park the car, and Bingham found the reception desk where a brief telephone call ensured he was not kept waiting long. A nurse – young, plump and smiling – welcomed him with a smile and a touch on his arm. He'd noticed that young people often behaved in that way, as though they felt he needed reassuring because of his age.

"Mr Bingham?" she asked, "I'm Staff Nurse Bakshi. We've managed to find a bed for your son," and then added, with a joyful laugh, "Is he always stubborn? He wouldn't consent to an operation until he'd seen you. Something about a dog. If you'll follow me."

Bingham did, pleased that his son had tickled this nurse's fancy and inherited the family streak of stubbornness, a streak inherited Bingham's father had always said from Bingham's mother.

His impression of the external appearance of the hospital was more than amplified as he followed the nurse along its corridors; not only did they sparkle with a cleanliness almost unbelievable in such a busy place, but the open aspect of the building illuminated them with daylight. Even on such a day, the rain running down the windows did little to disturb the effect of the light that poured in through the glass. At strategic points, hardwood seating was positioned, presumably for visitors waiting outside a ward or clinic, and broad dado rails prevented damage to the pristine green and light grey walls. Cleanliness and its relationship to godliness occurred to Bingham.

He found his son in a side ward at the far end so that the chair Bingham was offered had its back to a wall. Bingham wondered, very briefly, whether Ben had requested this consideration with his father's deafness in mind. Ben lay on his back, his leg elevated in a sling packed with ice. A doctor, who Bingham assumed had just arrived judging by the notes he was perusing and the expression on his face, looked up as the nurse and Bingham entered.

"Ah, Mr Bingham Senior," he said with a smile, "I am Dr Agarwal. Your son would like a quick word – and it must be quick. He has a compound fracture of the right fibula and we need to attend to his wound. Plates and screws are the order of the day! He has been given an anti-biotic injection and a tetanus shot and, as you can see, we are applying ice to help with the pain and keep the swelling down. He did consent to an MRI, which was nice of him. I'll leave you with the nurses, but don't be long."

The man's tone, which some might have considered to board on the sarcastic was anything but: a sense of humour seemed to be a requisite of the staffing.

"The staff have been wonderful, Dad – most considerate. I left Mollie with the man who was kind enough to bring me here. She didn't like it and I expect she's giving him a hard time. He has her in carpark H."

"What happened?"

"I did as you said and got chatty with the staff – casually as any walker knowing what had happened in Upton might – but either I handled it badly or simply picked a bad day or – and I think this more likely – one of the staff reported me to the hotel owner. He's a big bloke, tall, heavy muscled and fat into the bargain. He didn't like what I was asking one bit and turfed me out. Told me to leave. Said that the town was fed-up to the back teeth with nosey parkers stirring up trouble. The matter was all said and done with, done and dusted. You get the tone?"

"Yes."

"I had no option but to leave and made my way back to the town. The road is narrow – barely a single track in places – and I heard this car behind us. I looked round. Mollie was trailing behind in that way of hers, sniffing at every plant on the walk, and she was right in his path. I ran and grabbed her and dived for the verge. We were lucky: the hedge was thin at this point. Mollie and I somehow broke through and I found myself on my back with her in my arms and the next thing I knew we were rolling into a field that sloped down to the river. It wasn't until I tried to stand that I realized I couldn't take the weight on my leg."

"The driver then stopped?"

"No, no! My rescuer was a man who came along a tad later, by which time I'd crawled back to the road. I don't know how I made it. I felt nauseous – I almost vomited – and my leg was numb with cold. This man helped me into the car and brought me here. He's the one looking after Mollie."

"I'm sorry to see you in this state, Ben. Thanks for thinking of Mollie before yourself. You'd better let these good people help you now …"

"No, no, Dad, you don't understand. It wasn't an accident. It was clear the driver had no intention of stopping."

"He set out to run you down?"

"I'm not sure whether it was me. I'm of the opinion he was out to kill Mollie. Had he hit her she wouldn't have stood a chance. He'd have broken her back, run her over and carried on."

"You think it was a warning?"

"Yes."

"You may be right, Ben. Thanks for your courage and bearing this pain. I'll leave you to the professionals, now, and fetch Mollie," replied Bingham and, turning to the nurse who'd brought him to the ward, said, "Thank you, Nurse Bakshi. My son and I are grateful."

"You're welcome."

"I'll be back later, Ben, and I'll phone your mother."

"Must you, Dad?"

"I'm sure there'll be a lack of forgiveness in the air if I don't, son," replied Bingham, with a laugh.

Bingham had concluded during previous cases that there comes a turning point in any investigation, a moment when all becomes clear or, at least, when the way to a resolution opens. This was such a juncture, only it wasn't a resolution he perceived: more a wilful determination to settle the issue once and for all. Had he realized what his single-mindedness would incur, he might have laced his anger with a degree of calm.

John Hayes was waiting for him at the main entrance, and Bingham filled him in with the details. The newspaperman smiled grimly, gesture enough to coincide with Bingham's feelings and acknowledge the similarity of their respective experiences.

"You're sure they were trying to kill you?" asked Bingham.

"Or do me a great deal of damage. Let's have a chat with the man who helped your son and is now looking after this dog of yours."

"You think ...?"

"Who knows?"

Both did, on meeting the man: there was no question in their minds that he had been sent to survey the damage. He was simply a local who met his brother at the Rambler's Rest once a week for lunch.

"It's nice to get away from our wives for a while," he said, "We enjoy the peace and quiet of each other's company, and who knows how long we've got at our age."

"You can't recall anyone leaving up to a quarter of an hour before you?"

"I'm sorry, really sorry, but I can't. We were talking."

"There must have been a disturbance because my son was turfed out."

"I really can't help you."

"You say you met your brother for lunch?" asked John Hayes.

"Yes, once a week."

"But you left long before lunchtime."

"Yes, yes," replied the man, who by now was quite flustered, "My brother's wife has a dental appointment today and she doesn't like driving anymore, and so, today, we met only for coffee."

"I understand," said Bingham, realising they were pressing a man who had already been helpful enough, "Thank you for assisting my son – you've probably saved his leg – and for looking after Mollie."

"Oh, that's no trouble. My wife and I have a spaniel of our own. We love dogs. Mind you, she's a sparky one – yours I mean, not ours. Penny is very quiet. Mind you, yours has that look in her eye!" replied the man, and he chuckled.

"John," said Bingham, as they walked Mollie to the newspaperman's car, "May I take it that you'd be happy to help out?"

"You certainly may."

"There's no chance, is there, that you'd wade through that mass of paperwork you brought and dig out anything you can on this hotelier."

"Reggie Morton's the man."

"See if he appears anywhere in the picture fourteen years ago. And the husband – Mark Bawley. I didn't know until this morning that she was married."

"Oh yes, Mark's a decent chap. He works as a surveyor in Stoke. He was questioned by the police at the time. They had him in the cells but not for long. Is there anyone else?"

"Walter Higgins. He …"

"I know Walter. He does the odd job for me. How is he involved?"

"I don't know that he is, John, but his van was seen by Raymond Dowdall near the river path on that day. And keep your eyes open for the name Baylis …"

"Who runs the flooring shop?"

"Yes. A youth threatened me on my first night here …"

"Matthew Newham, who works for Baylis."

"Yes. You see, John, you must have been very near the truth of this scrambled matter for someone to be frightened enough to want to harm or possibly kill you. I'm off to see a man called Gerald Osman …"

"Lives in a rundown house up near the quarry."

"So, I'm told, and he appears on both lists: Roberta Dowdall's and Lauren Hagley's. I spoke with her this morning. She's frightened but keen to help. She wants her name kept out of harm's way. We could be barking up many wrong trees, John. I hope I'm not wasting your time."

"I've already spent years on this case – on and off – and nothing would bring me greater pleasure than to bring it to an end, but be careful, George."

"And you."

The two men shook hands in the custom of their generation, but there was more than a hug in their feelings, as they parted company at The White Hart:

John to review his research over the years, Bingham to phone Lina.

'Rundown' was a mild description, Bingham considered, for Gerald Osman's house. The hamlet in which it was situated must have housed, at one time, the families of the men who worked at the quarry, but most of them had long been forsaken for more modern properties in the neighbouring towns and villages. A lick of paint would merely have emphasised the dilapidation: tiles off the roof, brickwork in need of repointing, window frames rotten, guttering choked and flooding, every surface marked with the dust of the quarry, dust that now ran in thick streams of rainwater. The present downpour might have cleaned the windows had it stood a chance against the grime of decades; it didn't, and peer as he might Bingham could see nothing through the panes of glass. He heard movement within and knocked at the door.

When it was answered, Bingham was surprised at the man's appearance; somehow, he'd expected it to match the neglected house, but Gerald Osman was dressed smartly. Moreover, rather than derelict, he looked fit and even sprightly: a tall, wiry man in his fifties, going grey but with a definite distinction.

After Bingham explained his reason for calling, Gerald Osman looked him up and down for a while and, finally, asked him in.

"Do you mind if Mollie comes with me," asked Bingham, gesturing to her.

"No, not at all. I can't say I like dogs, but we can't leave her out in the rain."

The room lacked a woman's touch – there was no doubt of the fact – but it was tidy, even tidier than a woman might have kept it, if not swept and polished clean. Bingham had no qualms about seating in the proffered chair or of accepting the cup of tea he was offered.

"Mrs Dowdall said you might be able to help," said Bingham, "She said you were neighbourly."

"Ah, I know Bobby and Sam," replied Gerald Osman, cautiously, "They've had a rough ride over the years. I met them shortly after the murder. I can't remember how it came about. I must have met them in town, I expect."

"Did you know Ray?"

"Only through Sam. He kept me informed as to how his boy was doing in prison."

"You'd never met him before the murder?"

"I expect I had, but I can't rightly remember exactly."

"Did you live in Upton at that time?"

"No, I've always lived out of town. I'm not one for too much company, if you take my meaning."

"How did you come to hear of Janet Bawley's murder?"

The question clearly took Gerald Osman back; the expression on his face changed from chumminess to suspicion.

"It was fourteen years ago," he said, quickly, "I can't remember exactly where I was at the time."

"You didn't hear it from the Dowdalls?"

"No – yes – maybe. Is this important?"

"Very."

"Let me get this straight, Mr Bingham. How is it I can help you?"

"If we're to get at any truth in this matter – whatever that truth may be – we need, first of all, to place people where that were on that day all those years ago – the years Raymond Dowdall has been in prison. Since we arrived, my son and I have spoken to a dozen or more people and we know where they were in terms of time and place. There are certain key figures in this story. Once we know where they were, we can begin to create the pattern of their movements. You see, Mr Osman, no one's invisible: wherever you are, whenever you are, someone sees you or, at least, knows you are there."

Bingham wasn't sure when he spoke what provoked this speech; it was only later, as he reflected, that he became aware it had been fermenting in his mind ever since his son spoke to him. The effect on Gerald Osman was as he had anticipated.

"I think you'd better leave, Mr Bingham. What you're doing sounds like trouble."

"But not for you, Mr Osman?"

It was a question and a gesture at a reassurance, however false. Bingham was determined to have their conversation out but with no authority to do so.

"What do you mean?" asked Gerald Osman, sitting back in his chair and taking a swig from his mug of tea.

"Where were you that day?"

"I'm not after looking for trouble, Mr Bingham."

"Of course not," replied Bingham, pleased that his stab in the dark had produced some result, whatever that might be.

"I've always been a bit wild. The police were always picking me up, but I always kept coming back to Upton."

"Spent time inside, did you?"

"About eighteen months, on and off. Nothing big. It was always the drink."

"And now you're on the wagon?"

"I haven't touched a drop for years."

"What do you do for a living?"

"I get by. I'm not on the Social. I don't take charity. I do a few jobs, here and there, for people who know me. I work alone, usually, and I live alone. I like it that way."

"Were you questioned about Janet Bawley's murder?"

"I don't think so. I don't remember. There was no reason, was there?"

"Wasn't there?"

"I wasn't about here then," replied Gerald Osman's, his face expressionless.

"So, you do remember where you were?"

Gerald Osman shrugged his shoulders.

"Did you know Janet Bawley?"

"Everyone knew Janet. I'd seen her about."

"Had you spoken with her?"

"When?"

"At any time."

"I suppose I must have done. I don't remember."

"Have you ever done any work for Reggie Morton?"

"Everyone's done work for Reggie, at some time or other."

"Including you?"

"Yes. I said – everyone!"

"Would that include Walter Higgins? His van was seen near the spot where Janet Bawley was murdered."

"Was it?"

"Did you know Walter at that time?"

"Probably. I'd heard of him."

"You never worked with him."

"No."

"Not even when he was working for Reggie Morton?"

It was yet another stab in the dark for Bingham: he assumed that Walter Higgins must have worked for the hotelier at some time or other.

"I've worked for a lot of people. I told you – that's how I get by."

"You've worked with them both?"

"Yes! On and off! Another cup of tea?"

Bingham smiled and nodded. He watched Gerald Osman disappear into the kitchen, remembering another occasion, on the Costa del Sol, when he'd let another suspect out of his sight and come to regret his decision. He heard the kettle re-boiling. When Osman returned, he had a packet of biscuits under his arm. He passed them across to Bingham with the mug of tea. He then spoke, as though getting a weight off his chest.

"Walter and Reggie knew each other. They were at school together. Them and Matthew Pretty."

This was a new name for Bingham; he remained silent.

"They've always been close. Local businessmen, you see."

"They'd help each other out?"

"Yes."

Gerald Osman looked at Bingham, but he read nothing in the expression on the man's face. He seemed eager to link the two men and had introduced a third. Why? Was this an attempt to pin the blame or, more simply, to throw Bingham off the scent. Whatever his reason, Gerald Osman was worried.

"You know Matthew Pretty as well?"

"Everyone knows him. He used to be 'a bit of a lad' with the ladies."

"Didn't we all," replied Bingham.

Gerald Osman laughed: a reaction Bingham wanted. He needed the man to relax if only for a time.

"Did you know he had a record?"

Bingham knew nothing, but realised, now he had another name to conjure with, that PC Choudhury would. Bingham decided to throw yet another suggestion into the pot.

"Forensic science has moved on considerably since the murder, Mr Osman. If this case is re-opened, as I hope it will be, the Scene of Crime people will be able to unearth much more than they were able to do fourteen years ago."

"You mean DNA?"

"Among other advances. Nowadays it's possible to identify a killer through hair, fibres, blood samples, skin caught under the fingernails of the victim, palm prints … I could go on, but you'll know from the newspapers that killers have been brought to justice long after they've forgotten the crimes they committed."

Gerald Osman's face was white. Bingham continued:

"Would you be prepared to give a sample?"

"Yes, I suppose so."

"And talk with the police?"

"There's nothing I can tell them, really."

"But if it would help the Dowdalls who you're friends with or *have been friends with since the murder*, then you would?"

Gerald Osman did not miss the emphasis.

"Yes, I suppose so. Wouldn't anybody?"

The two men shook hands on Bingham's departure, Bingham elated, Osman taciturn. As he drove away, Bingham looked back and saw the man watching him from his battered doorway, the expression on his face saying he wished they'd never met.

"Bing, will you come and get me? I'm at the hospital."

Bingham picked up his wife's voicemail message when he arrived back at The White Hart and drove immediately to the Royal Stoke. It was dark and rain was still streaming down; rivers were beginning to overrun their banks and water was flooding the streets and the houses of those settlements unfortunate enough lie close.

Lina climbed into their car, shaking droplets from herself as she did so. Mollie demanded her attention from the back seat and then she turned to her husband, first kissing him and then sharing her fears.

"Ben seems comfortable, Bing, but the staff couldn't be sure he'll be free of any long-term complications. There could be permanent damage to the nerves and blood vessels around his ankle."

"Was he awake enough to tell you what happened?"

"Yes, but groggy after the anaesthetic. I regret persuading you to come."

"I believe you said the break would do me good."

"It's not funny, Bing. I just thought that you looking into this business would put Ben's mind at rest."

"I know," replied Bingham, removing his left hand from the steering wheel and rubbing his wife's thigh, "and I don't think Ben regrets coming."

"You're not giving up then?"

It was a question Lina needed to ask; she felt obliged to be the voice of concern and common sense but knew her husband's answer before he spoke.

"I think Ben's right in believing they were out to kill Mollie. It was a warning."

"I'm staying until he's fit enough to come home."

"I don't think that will be long."

"The staff nurse told me that they will provide him with a fracture boot until they are sure the bones are realigned. He'll be off work for weeks or even months."

"I don't think so. He's our son. He'll be back within a week of arriving home. Taxi to work and a wheelchair when he gets there."

Lina laughed despite herself. Her husband had caused quite a stir at his school when he discovered that a member of staff had taken three months off work because of a leg fracture but was able to drive from Ipswich to Bath each weekend to see her boyfriend. The headmaster had warbled something about 'health and safety' and refused to take any action, whereon Bingham, as head of the mathematics department of which the young woman was a member, had spoken with the teacher concerned. The resultant furore obliged the teacher to leave in the end, but only after taking "the sickness leave owed to me". Bingham had remained convinced that the school owed her nothing.

"Is there anything I can do?" asked Lina, "Apart from visiting Ben, I mean."

"Yes, there is – if you'd like to do so tomorrow."

"Anything."

"There's man who lives in Upton called Walter Higgins. Raymond claims to have seen his van parked at the junction near the murder scene on that day. Pay his home a visit, preferably when he's at work, and get chatting to his wife, Milly. Let her know who you are and what has happened to Ben. Use the line that we're trying to clear things up. If possible, take a gander at any photographs she might have on her sideboard – or wherever she keeps them. Note any of Walter, in particular. I'd like to know what he looks like."

"Do you know the address?"

"No, but he's a local handyman. He's well-known and it will be easy to find out where he lives. I heard about him at the hairdressers."

"I thought you'd had your hair cut. Unlike you, away from home."

Lina said nothing after that and they drove on in silence; she could see that her husband, as well as having to concentrate on steering their way through flooded roads and driving rain, was still struggling to place the events of that fatal day fourteen years ago into perspective. Besides, she had her youngest child on her mind and was worried sick about him.

It was 4 o'clock the following morning when Lina's phone rang. She and Bingham had both woken early, unable to sleep easily in a strange bed, and he was making them both a cup of tea.

"It's Phil," she said, "I asked him to keep an eye on the house and the animals. He seems upset – agitated might be a better word."

Phil Bassett and his wife, Maureen, were friends of the Binghams. They lived in the same village and he had introduced Bingham to beekeeping. Phil was always ready to look out for their pets (they had four dogs in addition to the thirteen cats that lived under the kitchen table), and he and Bingham shared a love of English classical music, particularly the works of Britten and Elgar. Bingham took her phone from Lina.

"George – is that you?" asked Phil, "There're some funny goings-on at your house. Some buggers are trying to set fire to it!"

Chapter Eight
A LOOK OF MELANCHOLY

"Bloody hell, George, I'll be buggered if I know what's a-going on."

'Bloody' and 'buggered', Bingham discovered on his arrival in Suffolk were common expressions among working men of a certain age; they were not to be taken as swearing, although it was unlikely the men would use them in front of their wives. They were often used during the working day and usually directed at inanimate objects rather than people; Bingham had heard carpenters direct them at furniture they were repairing, painters at gables they were preserving and electricians at wiring. On occasions he'd heard the term used in the home when children were referred to as 'little buggers', this being a term of affection for children who were mischievous; and the expression 'I'll be buggered' was used at times when they were pleasantly surprised by an outcome or occasion such as a friend doing well or an engagement being announced.

On this occasion, however, Phil was disturbed and angry, even frightened, and Bingham listened intently.

"I went up to the house to settle your animals and check things were all right, as usual, and I thought I'd take the dogs home with me for the night to save me worrying. O' course, that Pippa was all right – Labradors 'll go anywhere for a biscuit, won't they? – and so was the Westy, George, but that Cairn of yours, Ben, he's a right little bugger, he is, and he wouldn't come, so I said 'right, stay on your own' and left him. He was giving me jip.

Anyway, round about 3 o'clock I wake up startled. Don't know why. I suppose I'd been worrying about that little fella all night. So, I comes up to your house and sees this van parked in the old farmyard and these blokes in front of your place lighting something in what looked like a metal container. I weren't sure what. 'Christ', I thought, 'what the bloody hell's going on here? I didn't know what to do at first, George, but I knew I had to do it sharpish. Those buggers meant business. I couldn't see your house burned down, not after all these years. I knew the place when Lina's dad ran the farm from there.

Anyway, I had your keys in my pocket and knew where you kept your father-in-law's old 410, and thought I'd scare the buggers off. So, I went in through the back door and got myself the shotgun and some cartridges. I weren't a minute too soon. It was like bonfire night out there in the front by Lina's garden and they looked as though they were about to shove these burning sticks through the windows and the letter box. So, I gave them a warning shot and told them to bugger off. That held them in their tracks, but they still had these sticks with that burning cloth round them in their hands. I could see that, now, in the firelight. I told them to drop them and clear out, while I reloaded. They laughed at me and told me to – well, I won't use that word! One of them turned his back and set about lighting another of them brands in the fire they'd got going. I could smell the petrol from where I stood.

I don't get angry often, George, as you know full well and Maureen, my wife, will vouch for that but I saw red. I knew me distance, retreated a bit, aimed to the side and I gave him the barrel of the 410 in his arse, hoping he'd ketch some of the lead. There's nothing like a bit of buckshot up your arse to make you squeal, and he did. That turned the tables, that did: the buggers knew I had the upper hand and dropped their firebrands. They couldn't see me, of course, and didn't know how well I was armed. So, I told them to kneel down and put their hands on the path. The bloke I'd peppered was still squealing and wriggling, but your house was safe and that was all that mattered. I left him writhing about on the gravel, slipped down quietly to their van and put another couple of barrels into their front tyres. They aren't going anywhere, believe me."

"Aren't?" asked Bingham, still holding the cup of tea, untasted, that Lina had finished brewing after he took the phone.

"That's right. I'm waiting for the police and ambulance to arrive."

"You phoned them?"

"I always have my phone with me, George. You know that."

It was true: on many an occasion in Phil's allotment shed, Bingham had been treated to a slide of Phil's beehives, all twenty of them, each shot from various angles. The humour of the memory did little, however, to ease his mind at that moment. Bingham had rarely felt so stretched at one and the same time in so many different directions. He couldn't leave Phil to face the consequences of his actions alone, and yet he couldn't leave his wife and injured son in Upton alone.

"Don't you worry about me, George," said Phil, as though reading his friend's mind, "I'll be all right."

There was a stubbornness about the Suffolk temperament that was almost beyond belief to Bingham. He'd noticed it in many of the villagers – especially those who worked in and around the countryside – and also in Lina's father, an ex-soldier and arable farmer who'd met Lina's mother in Italy when the Allied forces made their advance through Italy following the routing of the Germans in North Africa.

"Phil, I'll get down there as soon as I can. If you need any help, contact our solicitors in Museum Street – you know Birketts – and thanks, Phil, from the bottom of our hearts. I don't know what to say …"

"There's no need for a fuss, George. The police know me. They're a-coming. I'll ring off now. Regards to Lina. Ooh, and don't worry about Ben. He'll come back with me this time whether he likes it or not. I can hear him barking, now. The little bugger hasn't stopped since I got here."

The phone went dead, and Bingham turned to his wife. She'd rarely seen tears in his eyes – once or twice, perhaps, when the children were seriously ill, or a pet died – but she saw them now and listened while he relayed Phil's account.

"Our home, Bing! He saved our home," said Lina, "Oh, what trouble is he in because of us?"

"We'll settle these people, once and for all," said Bingham, quietly, now recovered, "I thought the tide had turned when they tried to kill Mollie and ran Ben down. Now I know it has and we'll have these buggers before the week's out."

Both ate their breakfasts in silence and barely tasted the food, unusual in two people who enjoyed eating and particularly so in Lina who took pleasure in cooking and was fascinated by the cuisines of the many countries they'd visited together.

It was she who made the first 'sortie', as she expressed her trip to Bingham, using language learned at her father's knee. The rain was still pouring down, spreading its load, splashing upwards from the pavements and down from the roofs. Lina pulled the collar of her raincoat closer to her neck and tightened her hat.

Lina was nearing seventy but upright in her bearing. She'd retained her mass of hair, once black as a raven but now white, since she refused to use dyes, and her strong features had never aged. Her skin was unwrinkled – a genetic characteristic she felt she'd inherited from her mother, Eva Marinacci – and the Italian nose was prominent over a wide mouth that turned upwards, habitually, at the edges. Despite having given up her career as an opera singer when their first child was born, Lina still cared for her voice and when she spoke it bore the vibrance it once possessed on the stage. The dark eyes added to her general appearance and she was sometimes described as 'formidable', although this was not a view shared by her husband or children.

She'd found the Higgins's house easily – a question or two at the Londis Village store and she was soon ringing the bell of a house along Ousel Lane that had once been small but was now extended upwards and outwards thanks to the skills of the owner, Walter Higgins. Lina noticed a conservatory off the rear of the house leading to which there was a parking space large enough for several vehicles, a space that was bare on that morning.

The door was opened by a woman in her late forties or early fifties placing Walter Higgins as thirty-something at the time of Janet Bawley's murder, if he was a similar age to his wife. Milly Higgins bore an unfriendly expression, contrary to the impression given of her temperament by the villagers, and she stared at Lina before feeling obliged to speak. Even then, she kept the door almost on the jar and was obviously keen to convey the idea that she was too busy to talk.

"He's not here," she said, eventually, "He's not home."

"It was you I wanted to speak with, Mrs Higgins – if I may?" replied Lina.

"Who are you?"

Lina felt embarrassed for the woman: obviously an honest soul who was hiding something, something that roused her disapproval. A look of melancholy pervaded her entire face.

"I'm Lina Bingham. My husband ..."

"He'll be home later."

"I only want a chat, Mrs Higgins."

"What do you want with my Wally?"

"His name was mentioned. His van was seen ..."

"He wasn't there. It's all lies."

"But they are persistent lies, Mrs Higgins, and my husband is trying to clear them up."

"He wasn't anywhere near there that day."

"Near where, Mrs Higgins?"

"Near where you said he was."

"It was lunchtime, Mrs Higgins. Perhaps he'd parked his van to have his lunch."

"Wally'd have come home if he was in the village, but he wasn't."

"So, where was he the day Mrs Bawley was murdered?"

"Miles away. He told me."

"So, you know where he was? That would be a great help, if you do."

Lina felt the questions coming from her mind, somewhere and somehow, but wasn't sure where or how; what she needed to do, what she was critically aware of was the fact that she had to keep this lady talking, had to gain her confidence, had to give her the reassurance she needed.

"You see, we need to explain why people are claiming his van was there," she said, and added, hurriedly, "when it wasn't."

"Wally was miles away. You're mistaken."

"Was he questioned about Mrs Bawley's murder at the time," Lina persisted, feeling that the police files might contain something useful if the door was slammed in her face.

"He gave a statement, I think, but so did everyone else."

"So, what did he tell the police?"

"I don't know. He never said."

"Did he go to them of his own free will?"

"Yes, I think so."

"And he told them he was miles away?" said Lina, amazed again at her determination.

"Yes, I think so."

"We need to put the record straight, Mrs Higgins. May I just step inside? It's very wet out here."

"I don't know if Wally'd like that."

Milly Higgins peered out of her front door and saw the rain bouncing off Lina's back as she stooped forward to shield herself from the downpour.

"All right, then, just for a minute. I haven't got long."

The front door opened on to what was clearly a living room. Lina stepped inside, removed her coat and shook it outside.

"Here, give me that. I'll see to it," said Milly Higgins, and she took the coat.

The room was as neat and tidy as Lina had expected, and on the sideboard were a dozen or more family photographs.

"Your family?" she asked, moving quickly across the room to take a look.

"Gone now. Making their own way. Wally and I are alone now. Can I get you something?"

"That's very kind, Mrs Higgins, but I've just had breakfast and I know you're busy. I don't want to take up too much of your time."

"I was having one myself."

"All right, then. Thank you."

While she waited, Lina remembered her husband's often shared belief that 'someone, somewhere, knows something: after time, memories are stirred, loyalties change'. It was clear that Milly Higgins had something on her mind and as soon as she'd settled Lina with a cup of tea and a digestive biscuit she spoke.

"People kept saying these things. People who knew nothing about it."

"They claimed your husband was there that day?"

"They claimed to have seen Wally drive his van up Longshaw Lane, away from where … from where … you know … it happened."

"And this was at lunchtime?"

"So, they said. But he told me he was nowhere near the village that day, and I believe him."

"Who were these people, Mrs Higgins? Was it just gossip?"

"It was a coachload of pensioners off to a fancy lunch somewhere or other. Somewhere posh like Chatsworth House, I expect."

"And they told this to the police?"

"Yes. Wally went of his own free will."

Lina realised why Milly Higgins kept repeating that phrase: it was reassurance that it was true.

"Did the coach driver confirm the story?"

"Why do you ask?"

"Because coach drivers tend to have a very precise knowledge of time. It's important, isn't it, that we get that right? It has to be at lunchtime."

"The police said it was nothing to worry about."

"They said that to your husband?"

"Yes. They told him they knew who'd done it, and it was all right. He needn't worry."

"Do you remember the name of the policemen who said this?"

"It was our local chap, Bill Charlton. He came around to see Wally just to make sure he was all right."

In the next half-an-hour or so, Milly Higgins repeated what she has said over and over again but nothing new emerged for Lina to report back to Bingham. When she finally emerged from the house on Ousel Lane, dark clouds filled the sky and it was still raining but the look of melancholy had lifted slightly from Milly's face, and Lina was pleased. She suddenly apprehended what it was about his investigations that pleased her husband so.

Bingham had spent the morning warm and dry in the bar of The White Hart with John Hayes who had spent the night poring through his chunky file, looking in particular for any references to Reggie Morton, the hotelier, and Gerald Osman, the handyman.

When he arrived, early but soaked through, Bingham relayed the events of the early hours.

"I'm not surprised, George, at what they were attempting to do – although the speed of their response certainly takes my breath away! When my enquiries were at their fiercest our offices in Uttoxeter were torched. Someone shoved burning rags soaked in petrol through the letter box. It set fire to the carpet and that day's mail, but no other damage was done. I removed all the paperwork on Raymond straightaway, which was just as well because after the arson attempt there were a few burglaries."

"Lina could have been asleep in the house for all they knew," replied Bingham, "and Ben, our Cairn, was there. Whoever it is that's on to us, John, they're people who are able to obtain the information they need very quickly."

"You mean your address?"

"Yes. It's not as though I'm well-known. Anyway, I'll fetch you a coffee and we'll get on. What do you have on these gentlemen?"

Once they were settled, John Hayes's manner was brisk and business-like; he had separated the relevant information from the main file and cross-referenced it, collating all he had, however unconnected it seemed, into one document. Bingham, who had come to loathe paperwork because of that imposed upon schools during his final decade in the education service, was relieved and said so.

"There was a time during the two appeals that I didn't sleep at night," replied John Hayes, "but let's get on with it. This account is from a woman who was having an affair at the time and didn't want to be identified.

'... I'd met a male friend after taking my children back to school when they'd had their lunch. We were making our way down to the lane round the back of the church. It's quiet there. Then we saw Raymond Dowdall eating his lunch and we avoided him and made our way by the little path to the New Road. It was when we got to the bottom of the New Road that we saw Walter Higgins's van, so we retraced our steps, intending to cut through the woods. I didn't want to bump into him because I know his wife. It was then we heard the voices. I swear it was Reggie Morton and Janet Bawley and they were arguing, although we couldn't hear what it was about. While this was happening, we saw Matthew Pretty making his way along the lane.

Well, we didn't want to get caught up in all those shenanigans and so we decided to make our way back up to the churchyard. It was when we *were there that Ken – he's the male friend I was meeting – happened to look over the wall and he saw Matthew Perry running back along the lane. I think it was Matthew Perry.*

We were undecided what to do. We'd usually had no bother along the lane because it's shielded from the road and after a little while I looked over to see if it was clear. It was then I saw Raymond Dowdall bending over Janet Bawley's body.

I'm writing this in the hope that you can clear the young man's name ...'

"The letter's anonymous, of course," said John Hayes, "and was, therefore, useless regarding an appeal. There were other witnesses at the time who claimed to have seen Higgins's van in the area."

"There's no chance the letter is a hoax, is there?"

"Malicious, you mean, to implicate people the writer doesn't like? I don't think so, but it remains a consideration. This next one is my notes from a phone call. I wrote it down as I listened to the speaker – another woman," said John Hayes handing Bingham a neatly typed sheet.

'Janet was known to me and I had seen her accompanied by a man along that lane. It was at this time she was visiting a farmer in the Peak District. I'd seen her with him on several occasions in his car.'

"You see the problem," said John Hayes, shrugging and smiling at Bingham, "but I've pulled this out of my file because it occurred to me at the time that it might have some connection with this letter."

The journalist handed Bingham another letter, which had been typed.

'I was helping out on Mr Pretty's farm at the time, helping his wife who ran the business side of things. Mrs Pretty became suspicious that he was involved with a very attractive young woman from Upton. She said her name was Janet Bawley. She asked me to keep an eye out and let her know if I saw them together. She thought her husband used to meet Mrs Bawley somewhere in the farm and she wanted me to keep a look out when I was driving around. I often used to see them together. Sometimes in his Land Rover and sometimes in the fields. One day I saw them kissing and I think he saw me watching. I was frightened after that. He kept staring at me as though warning me to say nothing or else. He was not a man you would want to cross. Quite a few local men would come to the farm for work and they were frightened of him. You could tell by their manner. I did not say anything because I did not want to end up like Mrs Bawley but I feel bad about it now and wanted to tell you what I know.'

"She refused point blank to meet me when I traced her," said John Hayes, "She said there was nothing more she could tell me, and she wouldn't make a statement. I tried to coax her, but it was no use."

"Do you know this Matthew Pretty?"

"We've met. What the woman said is true. He's got some big friends: men who might enjoy a spot of bother. He seems to have some kind of hold over them. They do odd jobs for him: building, driving, deliveries – that sort of thing."

"Have you anything on Gerald Osman or Reggie Morton?"

"I might have," replied John Hayes, "Sometime after I retired, I received a phone call from a man who wanted me to meet him. He was adamant that I came alone and without any tape recorders or cameras. I was suspicious, of course: I'd been lured to out-of-the-way places before, but I went. It was an area that had been deserted for years. Once a place popular at the weekends for boating and picnics it was now overgrown and derelict.

When I got there, I saw this man sitting on the edge of the river throwing stones into the water. There didn't seem to be anyone else about and so I approached him. He didn't even turn around let alone look up at me. He just said: 'Are you the newspaper man?' and then went on to say he knew who had killed Janet Bawley.

He was a rough looking character and I was very uneasy, but he had my attention. He got up after he'd made that statement, walked to the water's edge and tossed a beer can into the river. He was obviously enjoying his moment. I noticed that he'd been drinking. There was beer cans scattered around where he'd sat. He talked on for a while about his own life and what a hard time he'd had – I received the impression he might have something seriously wrong with him – and then he got to the point.

At one time he'd worked for Reggie Morton as a barman and got to know him quite well. Reggie, evidently, had an eye for the ladies and was keen to boast about what he called his 'conquests'. He preferred women who liked it 'a bit rough' and there 'was no shortage of them'. He and Gerald Osman used to pick up hitchhikers and, if they seemed keen, would give them a 'good time'. Sometimes, they'd approach women they met at motorway cafeterias. Reggie reckoned you could always tell the type he and Gerald Osman preferred.

I got the impression that this character and Reggie spent time together chatting after the hotel had closed at night, while they cleared the bar. Alcohol certainly loosened Reggie's tongue because he claimed to know who had killed Janet Bawley. He boasted that the real killer would never be caught because he was too clever and had a 'friendly copper'. He said that Gerald Osman was the one who finished her off, and that he'd boasted about it. Reggie said that 'she had it coming to her', 'she had herself to blame' but it was a shame because 'she was a good sport' and he'd given her a 'good slapping' on more than one occasion. Another world, isn't it, George?"

"Yes, and not a very savoury one," replied Bingham. "I take it that you didn't get this man's name."

"No, and to be honest I saw no point in tracking him down. It was all talk, mostly as a result of drinking too much, and none of it amounted to evidence. But it did point in one or two directions and opened up a line of enquiry I was half expecting."

"The 'friendly copper'?"

"Yes, and I've no doubt who he is."

"PC Bill Charlton."

"You've come across him?"

"I've heard him mentioned. Did this character have any idea as to why Janet Bawley was murdered?"

"He thought about that long and hard but the best he could come up with was that she'd become some sort of liability. He said she had refused to keep her mouth shut over something important and kept repeating that she had information that could 'bury Reggie'. He kept saying that others were involved. What he said threw an unpleasant light on Janet Bawley's character, of course."

"First, know your victim if you want to solve a crime," replied Bingham, "I've spoken with a friend of Mrs Bawley's and what you were told fits the picture."

"At the one of my submissions to the Home Office, it was pointed out by an Under Secretary that (what did he say exactly? Oh yes) 'the information provided is at best speculative, as is the suggestion that one of her male friends might have attacked her'."

"Nevertheless," said Bingham, "you thought, quite rightly, that there were grounds to justify a closer look at each of them."

"Yes."

"Have you anything else, John?"

"There is the conversation I had with a local businessman just before I retired. I'd only been home from work for an hour or so and Joan and I were settling down to watch the television when the phone rang. Joan answered and said it was a man who wouldn't give his name but had information about the Dowdall case. He needed to speak to me urgently. Joan wanted to put get him to phone me at work the next day, but I was curious. We'd been ex-directory for some while following a series of threatening calls and I wondered how he'd found our number.

The man had a deep, gruff voice and he sounded very cautious. Asked me if I was John Hayes of the Uttoxeter Herald, said he was a 'friend of a friend and that some of the people concerned with Janet Bawley's murder were customers at his business in Stoke.

He wanted to meet me that night. Joan was against it and said I shouldn't go out, it could be a trap, but he insisted he wouldn't come to the newspaper office and I felt I had no choice. He wanted to meet in a pub at Stone. I knew it well and thought it a safe spot. Joan was angry, I can tell you, said I was stupid even to think about going out that late and so on, but I went.

I bought a coke and sat myself down when I got to the pub and no sooner had I done so than this man walked in. He recognised me because he walked straight over to where I sat. He was a tall, thick-set man. He got himself a beer and offered to buy me a drink, but I don't drink and drive and just indicated he should sit down. I'd chosen a seat in the corner where we could talk more easily.

He got to the point immediately. He said that Gerald Osman had attacked Janet Bawley on the river path. He had heard him, Reggie Morton and Walter Higgins boasting about it at his premises in the town, over a fairly long period of time."

"What premises were these?"

"He runs a restaurant in the town."

"Did he tell you that?"

"No, I took the trouble to find out."

"But you never sought him out there?"

"No, a promise is a promise."

"Quite!" replied Bingham, who had made some odd promises to villains in his short time as an investigator, much to Lina's disapproval, "Go on, John."

"He also brought in the name of Matthew Pretty."

"The farmer whose wife thought he was having an affair with Janet Bawley?"

"Yes. He went on to say that the conversation became more and more intense over time – probably as I pushed for reviews of Raymond's case. I also found out from Raymond's father that Gerald Osman had struck up a friendship with the Dowdalls soon after the lad's conviction."

"Yes, I put that to Osman, but he was evasive."

"Sam Dowdall said that Osman took a great interest in their protestations of Raymond's innocence. My informant kept looking around as we spoke. He was obviously nervous and fearing for his livelihood. He told me that a friend of his…"

"The friend of a friend?"

"Precisely! This friend told him that he'd heard Osman boasting that he'd 'finished the bitch off'. I had all these parts of a puzzle buzzing round in my head, George, but nothing solid to take my investigation forward. You'll appreciate that in a small community where people are interrelated or close friends or neighbours that it's difficult to make rapid progress. I wasn't sure from what he was saying whether the killer had acted with another man or had been hired to kill Janet Bawley. But I did, during our conversation, become convinced of two things: firstly, at least two people were involved in the murder in some way or other, and secondly, that these people knew Raymond would be eating his lunch in the churchyard at that time. He was a lad with learning difficulties, shall we say, and would make what the Americans call a fall guy – an excellent fall guy. It would be very easy to place the blame on Raymond and very difficult for him to express his innocence, especially if he was interrogated by someone who knew the result they wanted."

Chapter Nine
REFUSED TO ANSWER ANY QUESTIONS

The two men sat quietly after John Hayes had finished his account, both realizing that they were up against the proverbial wall of silence, an experience with which the newspaperman had been familiar for the previous six years during his investigations into what had seemed to him to be a miscarriage of justice of the first water.

Bingham reflected, not for the first time since he'd arrived in Upton-on-Churnet, on the difficulty faced by the police force in any investigation; they were dealing all the time with liars of one sort or another: those who falsified the truth, those who shied from it, those who hid it.

John Hayes's thought was, perhaps, less charitable towards the local constabulary; in his view they – or, at least, a few of them – had deliberately perverted the course of justice. They were the reason Raymond Dowdall had spent fourteen of his thirty-one years lost to the world, behind bars for a crime he did not commit. They were the ones who had falsified the truth, much as criminals do, for their own ends.

Bingham, at home in the bar of The White Hart and treating it as such, made them both another cup of coffee, while they waited for something to happen or for one or the other to speak. They were both old men, content in their silence and the reflections it engendered. In his seven previous investigations, it was at such times Bingham had suddenly had a shiver of apprehension that led him on, a frisson that opened the door to the light.

It was as they sat waiting that the door of the pub opened. Standing with the rain behind her and dripping from her coat was Mehreen Choudhury, briefcase in hand, not in uniform but in the traditional costume of her race, the salwar kameez, revealed as she removed her coat and hung it neatly from the rack. She smiled and Bingham thought he'd rarely seen such beauty in a stranger.

"I thought you'd like to know how your friend is faring in Suffolk," she said with a smile that Bingham feared might be inappropriate, "Yes, I'm off-duty," she added, probably in answer to the look both men were giving her.

"Thank you," replied Bingham, "Can I get you a coffee?"

"Thank you. On such a day it is welcome."

There was something about the way she spoke – the turn of phrase, the intonation – that removed the young woman from her role as an officer of the law, and yet Bingham retained his initial doubts. Was he being helped or was he being watched?

She sat waiting quietly at the small table where the men sat by the window that overlooked the High Street of Upton, her right leg crossed over her left knee, the gold and black of her costume (and Bingham could not but help thinking of her clothes in that way) dappled in the light of the raindrops that clung to the pane, until Bingham had placed the coffee before her.

"The three men refused at first to identify themselves and one has remained obstinate after several hours of questioning, but we managed to convince two of them that it was in their best interests to co-operate with us. They are Walter Higgins and Martin Newham ..."

"Oh no," cried John Hayes, "always the small fry who carry the can. The third is a tougher character, I imagine, isn't he – big, muscled, looking for trouble?"

"The Suffolk police might describe him that way," replied Mehreen Choudhury.

"You'll get nothing from him," said John.

"The other two insist that it was not their intention to burn Mr Bingham's house to the ground. They were to stand in front of the house with the firebrands in their hands and have their photograph taken. This was to be a warning to Mr Bingham not to interfere in the Dowdall case."

Bingham laughed. He couldn't help himself and neither could he control his mirth when John Hayes joined him. The young police officer may have had a twinkle in her eye, but laughter was not in her report book. She waited until the men calmed down.

"They did have a camera with them," she said, still apparently amused but without a smile.

"Did they mention who had sent them to be photographed?" asked the newspaperman, still repressing laughter.

"They refused to say."

"Terrified they might be *warned* themselves, no doubt."

"And Phil Bassett?" asked Bingham.

"He must be charged, Mr Bingham. He shot at one of the men ..."

"Which one, as a matter of interest?"

"The one Mr Hayes described as big, muscled and looking for trouble."

"Good, at least some just desserts are on the table," said John Hayes.

"Phil was only *warning* them," said Bingham, "in much the same spirit as the youth warned me, Reggie Morton arranged to have my dog run over as a warning but seriously injured my son instead and someone – as yet unknown – arranged to have my house photographed."

"None of what you say can be proved, Mr Bingham. In this instance, the man was injured and even if does not prefer charges, we will be obliged to do so."

"Some years ago, a case came before the courts," said John Hayes, "A farmer had seen what he claimed he thought was a rabbit in his wheat field, but which turned out to be the backside of a man having sex with a girlfriend. The famer opened fire and peppered the lover's rear with shot. The man claimed the farmer knew exactly what he was shooting at and did so deliberately. I forget what happened for the moment, but I'll look it up. I remember reporting it at the time."

Bingham laughed but Mehreen Choudhury looked at the two old man, obviously wondering if they came from another world or even another planet.

"Will they be released?" asked Bingham.

"Certainly. We have no reason to remand them in custody, but charges will be preferred, and they will answer in court for what they've done ..."

The policewoman paused, quite deliberately, holding the attention of the two men who realized she had more to say.

"I believe you will be interested in what else I have to say, gentleman," she continued, and proceeded to take a file from her briefcase, "I have spoken with a former police officer. He was a young constable at the time and with a view to retirement does not want to lose his pension entitlement, which he feels will happen if he talks to the press, and he is concerned about breaching the Official Secrets Act. You understand he will not make a statement or corroborate anything I have to tell you?"

"Go on," said Bingham, in a manner described, at times, by his family as 'abrupt'.

"This officer was involved with the initial interrogations and had access to the Prosecution file at the time of Mr Dowdall's trial. What he noticed was that there were about a dozen witness statements from police officers who did not exist. These statements were neither signed nor dated. There were other statements, too, from officers who had, clearly, not taken the details. He queried a statement by one officer, which did have his name and number on it but which he denied signing. Moreover, he denied writing the statement.

This police officer, who is an inspector now, advised my informant, at the time, to leave well alone when he challenged him, saying there had obviously been a mistake."

"But it was no mistake, was it?" said John Hayes, "It was all part of a cover-up that gave alibis to people who might otherwise have been questioned. Was Reggie Morton really questioned, was Gerald Osman, was Matthew Pretty, was Walter Higgins?"

"No," replied Mehreen Choudhury, "and there's more. After my informant had spoken with the officer concerned, he received a visit from a detective superintendent. The man barged into his office, pushed him against the wall and arm-locked his throat. The detective said that he hoped my informant wasn't 'hoping to get that little shit Dowdall off the hook because the shit would hit the fan if he tried'.

"What did he do?" asked Bingham.

"He made a report to his commanding officer but heard nothing more."

"Who was the detective involved?" asked John Hayes.

"Detective Superintendent Taylor."

"I came across him some time ago. He's retired now, of course. I didn't know about this assault on the young police officer, but Taylor told me quite categorically that a great many of the issues the Dowdalls and myself were raising had been dealt with at the time."

The silence that followed Mehreen Choudhury's revelations overshadowed even the one that had hung between the two men when she arrived at The White Hart: so much information, so little they could use.

The emotions running through the two men were doing so simultaneously: anger and frustration mixed with admiration for the young police officer who had, they had no doubt, put herself into a difficult, possibly career-threatening, position. The question they both wanted to ask had still not been spoken when the pub door opened, and another woman walked in; this time it was Lina.

Sensitive to the atmosphere, she smiled but said nothing and stood quietly dripping water onto the floor. It was Bingham who moved first, introducing the two women and then taking his wife's coat to the rack.

"Coffee?"

"Are we supposed …" Lina began, and then looked at the cups on the table.

If his wife had a fault, Bingham thought, it was worrying too much about what others might think and whether they should be doing something inappropriate: in this case, helping themselves to drinks in someone else's house.

While Bingham fetched her coffee, Lina sat in admiration at the Bangladeshi woman's clothes. The pattern along the hem consisted of a series of shapes that might have been abstract representations of human beings or symbols of the sun itself, so intricately interwoven in golden thread against the black that it was difficult to tell.

"So beautiful," she said, "I could imagine wearing your dress on stage."

The police officer smiled, lighting the moment and the bar.

After Lina was settled with her drink, she shared what she had learned from Milly Higgins and Bingham summarised what Mehreen Choudhury had told them; and then Lina asked the question that had silenced the men.

"What are you going to do with the information you've discovered, Mehreen?"

"I know what I should do."

"Be careful," replied Lina, "Every police force in the world needs people like you. Don't jeopardise your future. Sleep on your decision."

'I'll sleep on it' was one of Bingham's phrases; he caught his wife's eye and smiled; she'd spoken his very thoughts.

Mehreen Choudhury smiled, noticing the look that passed between husband and wife. Not wishing to pursue the question of her decision, she changed the subject.

"You will be visiting your son this afternoon?"

"You know about Ben?" asked Bingham.

"Hit and run accidents are reported automatically by the hospital, and your name is high on our list of concerns, Mr Bingham. It attracts attention."

"I'll visit this afternoon, Bing. I imagine you have something to do," suggested Lina.

The young woman's eyes widened; she wondered whether all married couples were telepathic.

"What is it you intend to do, Mr Bingham?"

"I imagine John and I will also be visiting," Bingham replied.

"If you've no objection, George., I'd like to take ex-PC Charlton. If I remember rightly – and I do – he was involved with the initial interrogations."

"My pleasure, John. I think Reggie Morton deserves my first visit."

"What do you hope to achieve?" asked Mehreen Choudhury.

"With what you've been able to tell us – and without revealing our source, in true journalistic fashion – we'll be able to shake these gentlemen up a little," replied Bingham.

The two women looked at Bingham, caution in both pairs of eyes: in one brought about through professionalism, in the other by love.

John Hayes had long wished to revisit PC Bill Charlton. 'Bill'! Such a friendly name, wasn't it? Anyone with a name like that could only be your chum. But was he a chum to Raymond Dowdall? He'd cropped up on and off throughout the years, especially in connection with the Raymond Dowdall's statement.

He'd been there at the beginning and they'd now discovered that it was at the beginning when 'about a dozen witness statements from police officers who did not exist' were made, 'neither signed nor dated'. Was PC Bill Charlton the 'friendly copper' Reggie Morton had boasted about?

John Hayes was looking forward to meeting him once again. A local copper, a man proud of keeping his patch crime-free, now retired but still living in Upton-on-Churnet in a nice, new little property in a cul-de-sac off Back Lane. How many 'Back Lanes' were there in Britain, thought John Hayes as he stood admiring the semi-detached house with its neat privet hedge dividing Bill Charlton's driveway from his neighbour's. Near enough to the town centre for the ex-copper to stroll to the local hostelries; far enough away to keep him clear of any current yobbos. What copper wanted to deal with them in his retirement? They'd given him enough headaches during his working life.

These were John Hayes thoughts as he knocked on the door, thoughts that might, during his working life, have formed the beginning of an article on a local character. The downpour had stopped, if only temporarily (John could see the black clouds still hung low), and so he had walked through the old market town, noticing, as Bingham had done, the orderliness, the neatness, the precision and the calm.

"No comment," said Bill Charlton when he opened the door and saw his visitor.

"I'm retired, PC Charlton."

"You people never retire. Leave me alone."

"You've been warned I might be coming, have you?"

"I don't know what you're talking about, and don't want to. Now – off!"

"It will only take a few minutes."

"It won't take even that! Off you go!"

"I won't keep you long."

"You can say that again," replied Bill Charlton.

As he spoke, he attempted to slam shut the door but John Hayes's foot was already on the step and so he couldn't quite close it. It was an old trick of newspapermen: forcing people to face questions on their front doorstep, where the neighbours might listen. Semi-detached houses are particularly susceptible to such a strategy and Bill Charlton opened the door.

"Come in and make it snappy. You've got five minutes. I know what this is about."

The lounge was immaculate; once placed in the preferred position, no object would have dared to move to another. The photographs on the sideboard were of a family: a mother, two children and Bill Charlton as a younger man.

"You're married, I see."

"Was – it didn't work out."

"So, you live alone now?"

"She had the kids and so she took the house. It was only after they left home that I could get my money back and put it towards this place."

"Nice," replied John, keen to put the policeman at his ease: people rarely tired of talking about themselves, "You decided to settle in the town where you worked for all those years?"

"I know the people and they know me. It makes for a quiet life."

"Do you ever see your children? I expect they've got lives of their own now."

"You haven't come here to chat about my children, Mr Hayes. What do you want?"

"Some more information has come to light …"

"It always and it always will. We acted on what we had at the time."

"It's that I want to talk to you about."

"You're running out of time."

"Do you mind if I sit down."

It wasn't a question and received no answer, and so John made himself comfortable in a chair by the electric fireplace and waited for the other man to sit.

"This is new information …"

"It always is! We went at length through the evidence at the time. We were left in no doubt about Dowdall's guilt."

"Had you come across him before the murder?"

John Hayes wasn't sure why he'd asked that question. Talking to Bingham later he expressed his puzzlement. Bingham smiled and said 'Intuition. I depend upon it all the time. Perhaps it was the way Charlton said the boy's name' and the newspaperman agreed this was so.

"You mean around the town?"

"Yes."

"Why do you ask?"

"If you knew of him, it would inform your judgement."

"Everyone knew of him. He was the awkward kid, the weirdo, if you like."

"Weird in what way?"

"Well, he's not quite right, is he?"

"Had he been in trouble before?"

"Let's just say we were waiting for him to do something we could catch him for."

"There was nothing said at his trial that suggested Raymond had anything but a clean character."

"Perhaps we hadn't got sufficient evidence to convict him."

"Do you hold yourself responsible for Mrs Bawley's murder?"

"What do you mean?"

"Well, if you had reason to suspect Mr Dowdall of something weird, you might feel that her killing could have been prevented if you'd caught him before."

"It was gossip, innuendo. We had nothing to get a conviction."

"What kind of innuendo?"

"I said – he was weird, and still is, as far as I know."

"His neighbours spoke well of him."

"They would, wouldn't they?"

"Was your view one shared by the force generally?"

"We all knew him for what he was."

Give a dog a bad name and hang him. Was it the old saying that informed their judgement? John Hayes could imagine this view of Raymond becoming police folklore. He could hear the comments when Raymond was brought in for questioning. Thinking back to when he'd read through the mass of 'evidence' the Dowdalls had collected, he recalled the neighbours saying that they'd been fobbed off with such gossip when they had contacted the police with potential information. The police had simply not wanted to know.

There was something else, too, in the Dowdalls files. What was it?

"Were you there when Raymond was questioned?"

"Among others."

No, no, thought John Hayes, suddenly recollecting what it was he half-remembered.

"You were the officer who took his statement, weren't you?"

"Yes. Look, Mr Hayes, I'm retired. I've had enough of these questions. It was all settled long ago. You newspapermen are like a dog with a bone. Let it go!"

"You were alone with him at times, weren't you? You stood in front of him and were very friendly. I believe Raymond said that you sounded like his dad. You said that if he told the truth things would be easier for him. That's the case, isn't it, PC Charlton?"

"If you say so. If, as the boy claimed, he and I were alone in the room only he and I would know that, wouldn't we. His word against mine. Besides, it isn't regular practice to be alone with a suspect, and so I expect he was wrong."

"You see, some of the statements made at the time have come to light and the funny thing about them is that not only are several of them unsigned but the people who made them don't even exist. What do you make of that?"

"I don't make anything of it. It isn't my business to. The jury must have been satisfied as to their authenticity at the time."

"If they saw them. There's another statement, perhaps a key one as far as the prosecution council were concerned, that is signed. This one was by a police officer – as, by the way, were the others I mentioned, the ones by the officers who didn't exist, only …"

John Hayes paused, seeing that Bill Charlton was getting hot under the collar; his eyes showed every sign of nervousness and evasion was written in every line of his face

"No comment. I can't say anything."

"…Only this one was signed and carried the officer's name and number …"

"Just go, newspaperman."

"The problem is – and judging by your face I think you know what the problem is ex-PC Charlton – the problem is not only does this officer deny signing the statement, but he also denies writing it. What do you make of that?"

"Out – you've had your five minutes and more."

"You don't think it possible, do you, that someone else wrote and signed it for him?"

Bill Charlton looked daggers.

"You see, this was a key prosecution statement. It might be argued when we bring this to appeal again – and we will – that perhaps, just perhaps, Raymond Dowdall's statement was written for him. He's a lad who had his difficulties at the time; perhaps someone gave him a helping hand. What do you think?"

Bill Charlton marched to his front door and opened it.

"I've got work to do. Since I retired, I do a bit for charity. It's a pity you don't make yourself useful in that way, instead of wasting people's time with a pack of lies."

Bill Charlton had told him nothing, he refused to answer any questions simply by challenging every point that the journalist made but as he left, and strolled off towards Back Lane, John Hayes was a very happy man.

Mehreen Choudhury had offered Lina a lift into Stoke and said she would drop her off at the hospital, and so while Lina changed out of her wet clothes Bingham had a few moments with the police officer.

"Will you have the chance to question Walter Higgins when he gets back to Upton?"

"Yes, I can arrange for that to happen. What is it you want to know?"

"Raymond claimed to have seen Mr Higgins's van parked on the road when he ran from the scene of the crime to fetch Mr Roberts. No one else mentioned this – *to be exact, there is no record of anyone else mentioning this at the time* – but Lina tells us that, according to Milly Higgins, a coachload of pensioners claimed to have seen her husband drive his van up Longshaw Lane, away from the scene of the murder. Mrs Higgins dismissed this as gossip and, according to her, so did the police."

"You want us to question Mr Higgins about this discrepancy?"

"Yes please. He'll be feeling very vulnerable now, as he's been charged with attempted arson. Press him hard – if you would be so kind."

Bingham added the final phrase when he noticed the frown on the young officer's face.

"Times have changed, Mr Bingham. These days we don't decide who's committed a crime and then get the truth out of them."

"No, of course not, I wasn't suggesting …"

"I know, but the point needed making."

Chastened but pleased, Bingham dressed for the weather and set off for the Rambler's Rest and his intended meeting with Reggie Morton, the man his son, Ben, believed had intended Mollie's corpse to be a warning. Mollie was with Bingham when he left, ambling by his side, her head occasionally tilted up towards him, watching his every move.

The rain had eased, and it was a long but pleasant walk. He came to the spot where the thin hedge was broken, the spot where his son had grabbed Mollie and dived for the verge. Bingham stood there for a while looking into the field that sloped down to the Churnet, the slope down which his son had rolled, dog in arms, to the river.

At the reception desk, he asked for Reggie Morton and the girl told him she would enquire whether Mr Morton was available because it was the lunch hour, their busy time.

"Mr Morton attempted to kill my dog and has crippled my son. He can see me in his office, or I can ask my questions from here. My voice carries; at one time I could be heard across the playground."

Bingham had never, ever, lost his temper, but that didn't mean he lacked one, and it carried in his voice. The receptionist's eyes popped wider; she didn't even wonder if he was joking.

When Reggie Morton appeared from a doorway that opened onto the reception area, he was everything Bingham had envisioned. He was, as Ben had described him, 'a big bloke, tall, heavy muscled and fat into the bargain'. Bingham also saw beyond the appearance. Reggie Morton was a bully, and like all bullies he had that weakness behind the eyes. Bingham had seen it on several occasions as a teacher. A parent would arrive, mother or father, and the bluster would begin. There was always a physical threat in their manner until they were challenged or calmed, and then they flinched, not bodily, perhaps, but in their manner and in their tone and in their eyes.

"Call the police, Dawn – NOW."

"There's no need," said Bingham, as the receptionist reached for the phone, "They know I'm here and will be along in their own good time, no doubt. I'm here to decide whether I press charges in the civil court as well as the ones you'll face in the criminal court. Do we talk here or privately?"

Reggie Morton hesitated, while the girl looked at him for advice, and then drew himself up to his full height, thrust out his chest and attempted to put a swagger into his voice.

"This way! Leave it, Dawn. I'll sort this!"

His office was crisp, minimalist and quite small: a mahogany desk with matching chair, laptop, telephone, two chairs facing the desk, a filing cabinet and a carpeted floor. There were no pictures on the wall nor photographs on the desk and no window although a light box gave the impression of one. Beneath this there was a settee of the Chesterfield type.

Bingham could well imagine Reggie Morton giving a woman 'a good slapping'. In his time, he had come across women who might have deserved one: a friend of his had been driven to suicide following twenty years of verbal abuse from his wife. But like Bingham, his friend had been of the old school: when it came to women, slapping was one line you didn't cross.

He settled himself into one of the guest chairs, indicated to Mollie that she should sit on the carpet by his side .and watched Reggie Morton, attempting to picture him at work and play. The hotel owner didn't sit, not at first: he stood and towered.

"Yesterday morning, my son, Ben, came to make a few enquiries regarding a murder that occurred here fifteen years ago for which a young man has been imprisoned for the past fourteen. You turfed him out and then sent a car to run him or our dog down. My son thinks you intended to kill Mollie as a warning to us to stay away from the Bawley case. I'm not so sure it wasn't my son you were after, but we'll wave that point for the moment. As it happens, my son was crippled by your driver, but you'll know this, won't you, Mr Morton? News travels fast between you and your friends, three of whom are now in the hands of the Suffolk police and will soon be questioned by the Staffordshire constabulary. Do you have friends in high places these days, Mr Morton, as you did fifteen years ago? Do you have a 'friendly copper'? You'll need one."

It was a long speech, which Bingham had been rehearsing as he walked; it was intended to shake the hotelier up, containing as it did several accusations and a dash or two of knowledge. Bingham knew Reggie Morton couldn't be sure whether that knowledge was possessed or assumed. It also implied that Bingham had a handle on circumstances the man would rather have kept concealed. Bingham was out to frighten him, to force the bluster. The man was a rabid dog. Would he turn?

"And you can prove all this – this fairy tale, this string of rubbish?"

"Enough to rouse interest in the rest. Your friends have already been talking and will be talking at greater length when the Staffordshire police question them. You see, Mr Morton, try as you might to conceal it, the truth will out in the end. Of course, truth is strange: it often seems to have two faces, or even three."

"What do you mean?"

"Is the truth we want it to be, the truth we scheme to make it? John Hayes's long campaign to get the truth for Raymond Dowdall will result in another truth – the identity of the man who really killed Janet Bawley. But will that be the whole truth and nothing but the truth or merely part of the truth. Will we imprison the wrong man again?"

"Have you finished?"

"It's never been established where you were on that fateful day, fourteen years ago, has it?"

"I was interviewed. It's in the statement."

"One of the statements that were neither signed nor dated made to police officers who didn't exist? You mean one of those? Or was it the one by the officer that did have his name and number on it but which he denied signing and denied writing?"

Reggie Morton sat down on his desk chair and leaned back. It was all he could do until his mind had worked its way through the string of rubbish the man opposite him was spouting. The case was watertight: gossips had been persuaded they didn't need to give a statement; the police side of things was sewn up nicely.

"It's surprising what people remember after fourteen years that they couldn't remember at the time," said Bingham, "Careless talk along the footpath of life – that sort of thing. People tend to recall the highlights – a row between lovers, for example."

It was stab in the dark, but a stab that came from Bingham's intense brooding on all he'd heard. Janet Bawley had walked happily to the copse but was dead within fifteen minutes; something had occurred previously that brought about her killing, and what more likely than a row.

Reggie Morton didn't flinch; he was too experienced at covering his own back for him to show any obvious emotion, but the remark went home. He looked at Bingham between half-closed eyes, wondering how much the man said was sheer bluff. Did he really know anything that hadn't been hidden years ago?

"You were at school with Walter Higgins and Matthew Pretty, weren't you?"

"What's that got to do with anything?"

"Old friends go back years, especially old friends who have lived in the same town all their lives, worked together, worked for each other, worked with each other. It brings a closeness, doesn't it? The writer, E M Forster, once said that if he was asked to betray his country or his friends, he hoped he'd have the courage to betray his country."

"What's that got to do with anything?"

It was the second time he'd made that response and Bingham realised he had his opponent on the ropes.

"When we spoke with Raymond Dowdall, we had all we needed to know within our sights without realising it," said Bingham.

"The kid's a weirdo and a liar."

"That's what Bill Charlton said when John Hayes questioned him this morning but it doesn't detract from the picture he painted, a picture in which each subject was perfectly placed if only we'd seen it, if only the police at the time had troubled to see it."

Another name tossed into the boiling pot of the hotelier's mind, another ingredient to unsettle him.

"It's a question of knowing who was where and why, isn't it – as I said to Mr Osman, when he was trying to place where he was that day."

"Gerry said you'd been poking around. Are you trying to tell me that he could remember that far back?"

"It isn't always a matter of what people can remember; sometimes, it's more a question of what they'd rather forget. You and Mr Osman are close, aren't you?"

"What do you mean?"

"You enjoy the same things, the same kind of women, good sports, those who like a good slapping?"

"Who have you been talking to?"

"Was Janet Bawley one of those?"

"She was a good sport. Nothing wrong in that as long as the woman enjoys it."

"Was she your lover?"

"That's nothing to do with you. We don't speak ill of the dead in Upton, whatever you might do where you come from, Mr Bingham."

He was retaliating; he was roused. Bingham smiled.

"Did you have a place in that little black book of hers?"

"I don't know what you're talking about."

"You must have come across quite a number of women in your time, Mr Morton?"

"I've had my share – and they've all been *good sports*."

"Married, are you?"

"No need! What would I want with a wife?" replied Reggie Morton with a loud laugh.

It was the first time he'd relaxed since he and Bingham began their conversation.

"John Hayes has been looking through his notes. It's surprising how something apparently insignificant can jog your memory. I just said to him 'Does the name Reggie Morton mean anything to you?'. It was after your attempt to kill Mollie, if – as my son believes – that was your intention. And suddenly, I saw the spark in John's eyes. The name 'Reggie Morton'. You might say it opened a window in the mind. John suddenly recalled someone he'd met some years ago – a man who's now down on his luck. It was all there in the notes he made at the time. This character told John he knew who'd killed Janet Bawley. Others had said the same, of course, and so John didn't get too optimistic at that time, but once other evidence came to light ..."

"What evidence?"

"Forensics," replied Bingham, surprising himself because science was the last thing on his mind at that moment.

"Forensics?"

"DNA – that kind of thing," Bingham continued, remembering how the very idea had startled Gerald Osman, "The man he spoke to was down on his luck, as I said. John thought he might be ill – terminally, perhaps – and wanted to get things off his chest. You know, clear his conscience before he met his god."

Bingham couldn't believe what he was saying. What had put that idea into his head? Was it something John had said?

"This character told John that you said 'She had it coming to her' in reference to Janet Bawley. You see, Mr Morton, one of the problems the police had was an *apparent* lack of motive for the killing. I stress the word 'apparent' because they might have found one had they looked closer. You take my meaning?"

"I don't think I do."

"Neither did the Home Office. They regarded the information as to Mrs Bawley's character as 'purely speculative', but we know differently, don't we?"

"I've had enough of this. You're waffling, groping in the dark, mate. Hop it! You know no more now than that nosy parker from the newspaper did years ago. I've a good mind to give you a bloody good hiding," retorted Reggie Morton, rising from his chair and leaning over the desk.

"I can see I'm not welcome here, Mr Morton, but before I go just one more point that might be in your interests to realise. Things are coming to a head and when they do people are going to apportion blame. I indicated a few minutes ago that truth is not an absolute: truth is what people perceive it to be or, more exactly, what they want it to *appear* to be. You'll know that because you know that Raymond Dowdall is innocent even though the *perceived truth* is that he's guilty of Janet Bawley's murder. There are key players in this murder, and you are one of them. Which of you is going to carry the can once we clear Raymond's name?"

Reggie Morton came around his desk, towered over Bingham and reached down for either his throat or his lapels; Bingham wasn't sure and wasn't to find out because then it was that Mollie intervened. She snarled and leapt at Morton who, instead of standing his ground, recoiled. It was a mistake because it gave the dog room to manoeuvre between him and her master. What might have happened never did because Bingham rose quickly and called her off fearing that she might savage Morton: an occurrence that would have pleased the man and his dog but spelled the end for her.

Reggie Morton reached back for the intercom on his desk, but Bingham stopped him by grasping the fat wrist.

"We'll call it evens for now, shall we, Mr Morton?"

"I'll have the police on you and your dog."

"I trust not. As your friendly copper, Bill Charlton, pointed out this morning, you and I are alone in the room, and only you and I would know the truth, wouldn't we? Your word against mine."

Bingham gestured Mollie to him and walked to the door, if the truth be known eager to leave before matters took an even nastier turn. He turned to Reggie Morton.

"Just one more thing, if you don't mind …"

"I do mind," yelled the hotelier, straightening his jacket and tie, "Get out."

"What did Walter Higgins carry in his van that morning?"

"Whatever he … How should I know?"

"I thought you might. Ooh, one last thing …"

"Get out! I shan't tell you again."

"I'd be obliged if you didn't send a car after Mollie a second time. That might …"

"I'll settle things with you, Mr Bingham, before the week's out."

"Good. I'm pleased to hear you say that Mr Morton. It's what I was hoping."

Chapter Ten
A LOT TO ANSWER FOR

When Bingham arrived back at the White Hart, Lina was sitting in the bar with a gin and tonic. John Hayes had been kind enough to go and fetch her from the hospital.

"How's Ben?" asked Bingham.

"Eager to go home, as you predicted. I thought he might stay with us for a week or two."

"That would be nice. He's good company but ..."

"... but, knowing Ben, he'll be eager to get back to work. I can complete the sentence for you, Bing."

"So, Ben said."

"Pardon?"

"Family habit," laughed Bingham, and Lina laughed, recalling the days when they were a proper family, meaning the children were children and all at home all the time.

"How did you get on?" asked John Hayes.

"I rattled his cage. No more. Were there times, John, when you felt really tired looking into Raymond Dowdall's case?"

"I know what you mean, George, but always the image of that lad locked in his cell for twenty-three hours a day came back to me."

"Yes. My head is simply bursting with details. Let me give you a condensed version of my meeting with Mr Morton. It may help to clear my mind."

"A beer?"

"Better not. We'll be going to the hospital soon for our evening visit."

When Lina and Bingham arrived, late because the driving rain had slowed their journey along the narrow roads that led to the A50, Ben already had a visitor. Roberta Dowdall was sitting at his bedside, profuse with her apologies, while Ben tried to reassure her that his accident was not her fault.

"I wish I hadn't got you involved, Mr Bingham," she said, catching sight of Ben's parents, dripping rainwater onto the ward floor.

"You didn't, Mrs Dowdall. Ben did," replied Bingham, smiling at his son.

"I'll go now, anyway. I've said what I came to say when I heard about the accident. I shouldn't blame you if you gave up now, Mr Bingham."

"There's no fear of my husband doing that, Mrs Dowdall," said Lina, "I'm Lina Bingham, by the way. We haven't been introduced. It's nice to meet you."

"Oh yes, I'm sorry," said Bingham, "Mrs Dowdall – my wife, Lina."

Roberta Dowdall offered her hand, but Lina simply moved forward and gave her a hug; hugging was a standard form of greeting with Lina. In these special circumstances, it was also a form of reassurance: Lina couldn't begin to imagine her own feelings should one of her children be imprisoned for a crime, let alone one she was convinced they hadn't committed.

"Nice lady," she said, taking the chair by her son's bed, while Bingham perched on the little storage cupboard next to the ward's wash basin, "I feel so sorry for Mrs Dowdall. How's she going to get home? Bing, do you think we should offer her a lift?"

"It's all right, Mum. Mr Dowdall is waiting in the car. He didn't like to come in. Mrs Dowdall brought some information I wasn't aware of, by the way. Did you know that Raymond Dowdall initially confessed to attacking Janet Bawley?"

"No," replied Bingham, his heart sinking just a little.

"You'll remember that Mrs Bawley was alive when the ambulance came. She died a few days later in hospital without regaining consciousness. Mrs Dowdall is convinced that her son was coerced into making a false statement because he thought it was the best thing to do at the time, believing that Mrs Bawley would tell the police what actually happened when she recovered."

"I should have read the paperwork," said Bingham, "The Dowdalls offered it to me but I was so tired on that first night I couldn't face it."

"That 'first night' was Thursday, Bing – three days ago! This is only Sunday. You haven't exactly been idle since arriving in Upton," Lina sympathised, going over to her husband and putting her arms around him.

"Don't blame yourself, Dad. Raymond retracted the statement a few days later when he realised the charge was murder ... But the original statement was used by the prosecution at his trial. It threw doubts on his innocence, of course. Raymond believed that someone would come along and save him. He never accepted that he would be convicted of a crime he didn't commit. It was only when he was charged with murder that he knew he had to do something to save himself. There was no agency out there to help him. According to Mrs Dowdall, he broke down and sobbed when he saw his father. He begged him to believe that he was innocent."

"The boy was tired, wasn't he? I remember, now. He said his dad came at about ten o'clock at night with some fresh clothes. He'd been questioned on and off since lunchtime. He was tired and hungry. 'He was in a hell of a state when I got there. He said he was cold and tired and that he'd had nothing to eat since lunchtime'."

Sam Dowdall's words came back to Bingham as he listened to his son.

"Mr Dowdall asked him where he'd been, and Raymond said: 'Here in this room'. He must have ached from head to foot, sitting on a hard chair for nine hours."

"Did he not have a solicitor?" asked Lina.

"Not according to Mr Dowdall. He asked if his son needed one and was told it was unnecessary because the police were only asking him questions."

On the way back to the White Hart, Bingham was silent and remained so while he and Lina undressed ready for bed. As he lay quietly by her side, Lina could tell that her husband was perturbed to the point of being dismayed. She reached across and took him in her arms.

"There was a time, Lina, when I could hold every little detail in my head. How else could I have taught children for forty years? Nowadays, I seem to forget as much as I remember."

"Does this latest information make any difference to the case, Bing?"

"I don't know – that's what troubles me. A pattern of events was settling into place in my mind. I'd said to someone, only this afternoon (at least I think I did, or was I only talking to myself?), that what Raymond Dowdall told Ben and I, when we visited him in Dovegate, painted the picture of events precisely. Everything was in place at that moment, in those fifteen minutes, if only we had recognised it, if only the police had taken the trouble to see it at the time."

Bingham slept uneasily that night; he removed himself from the bed, in case he disturbed Lina, and sat by the window. Monday morning came around to find him tired and worn down. It was the Monday of the November that experienced more rain than any Monday for the past fifty years. When Lina rose and made them both a cup of tea before they dressed, she saw the rain slamming at the window, with Bingham staring through it at an occluded world. Even in their room, with the central heating high, it was cold.

During breakfast, Bingham remained silent and Lina respected her husband's mood. She knew that he and John Hayes were faced with a busy day: they'd made their arrangements the previous evening.

When his phone rang, Bingham seemed not to hear it and so she reached across and lifted it from the table, but the caller wasn't the newspaperman.

"Bing, do you know a Mr Lean? He says he's ringing on behalf of PC Choudhury."

"Good morning. Mr Lean? How can I be of help?" said Bingham.

"Dr Lean, Mr Bingham. Mehreen Choudhury asked me to get in touch with you, Mr Bingham. I'm from the Forensic Laboratory in Nottingham. It's about the Dowdall case. Are you free to listen?"

"Yes, but I'd rather speak face to face. I loathe conversations on the phone. Can I come to you?"

"You could, but I've nothing on at present, Mr Bingham. I'd be more than pleased to come across to Upton."

"That's very kind of you. Thank you."

"In an hour?"

"That would be good. I'll look forward to seeing you."

When the forensic scientist arrived, he found not only Bingham and Lina but also John Hayes waiting for him. He was an elderly man, white haired and what the gossip columns like to call 'distinguished'; tall and portly, he made an impressive figure in the small bar. He shook his raincoat violently on the floor and hung it, together with his fedora, on the rack.

"David Lean – don't say it, everyone else does! I've never made a film in my life and wouldn't know where to start but I do admire my namesake. Mr Hayes – we have met."

"I remember," replied the newspaperman, his voice carrying a disgruntled note.

"We can only provide our evidence, Mr Hayes. What the court makes of it is down to them and the judge's advice to the jury."

"Hmm!" was all John Hayes seemed able to muster.

"May I?" asked the scientist, sitting himself across the table from Lina, after Bingham had introduced his wife and taken charge of the coffee machine., "I'm rather pleased this case has risen from the dust of the ages. Young Mehreen is a bright spark. We must hope she doesn't set light to herself."

His comments only enhanced his presence and the fact that he had taken command of the situation. Bingham admired him but cautiously. There was something of the que sera, sera about the man, a quality of which Bingham disapproved entirely.

"There was some disagreement at Mr Dowdall's trial regarding the blood stains on his clothes. I was of a different opinion from my colleagues, but their view won the day.

The patterns of staining on Mr Dowdall's trousers and fleece were consistent with what he had to say, that he'd knelt by the body to see if the lady was still alive and turned the body over. There was a deep stain on the right knee of the trousers and a footprint on the inside of his fleece, which he'd placed aside.

Where we differed was in the matter of the blood spots on the front of the shirt and the tie. They felt that these were not consistent with turning someone over. My colleagues were of the opinion that these could not have been occasioned when – as Mr Dowdall claimed – the lady sat up suddenly and shook herself before collapsing again. They did not accept Mr Dowdall's explanation that these small spots of blood flew on to his clothing when the lady shook her head. For that to have happened a great deal of energy would have been required; this was not consistent with the lady collapsing immediately afterwards. The splashes were small, you see, and my colleagues preferred the explanation that these had been brought about when the lady was attacked and beaten violently; the harder you hit, the smaller the spots."

Bingham had listened with feelings of wonder and horror, but it was the latter emotion he saw on Lina's face. She rose from the table and walked away from the men to peer out of a window still swarming with raindrops. It wasn't the explanation that had disturbed her so much as Dr Lean's matter-of-fact tone; Bingham knew this, while accepting that work like the scientists' required a great degree of objectivity and not a small amount of black humour. He looked across at Lina, but her stance told him to stay put.

"I'm sorry," said David Lean, "I had no desire to upset the lady."

"No, it's quite all right," replied Lina, "please carry on."

"Yes, please do," urged Bingham, remembering what his son, Paul, had suggested to Ben: 'the only way Raymond's clothes could have been splattered with blood as they were would be if he had struck the blows'.

"However," continued Dr Lean, "I disagreed. I felt then, and still do, that the blood splashes on Mr Dowdall's shirt and tie could have resulted from the lady shaking her head, if the shakings were violent enough. You will remember from his statement that Mr Dowdall said she sat up suddenly and seemed disturbed by some movement or other from the copse where, presumably, she might have been attacked. Her heart was still pumping at that stage. You may also remember, if you've examined the case notes, that the young policeman and the ambulance driver both described her as shaking her head 'aggressively' – that was their word for it.

Overall, I felt that the bloodstaining was consistent with Mr Dowdall's version of events."

"Just a moment," said Bingham, quite distracted.

"I beg your pardon?"

"Just a moment. I need to collect my thoughts. My older son is a doctor. He gave us a similar view to that of your colleagues. Let me just think for a moment what he said to my son, Ben."

Bingham rose and walked across the bar, desperately searching his memory, angry with himself for the time it took.

"It will come to you, Mr Bingham. At our age recall is slow."

It was a kind remark and meant kindly and Bingham smiled his thanks to the scientist but was acutely aware that this man had just recalled in considerable details events from fourteen years ago. Bingham felt old and frightened. What if he couldn't remember?

"Paul was cautious," he said, at last, with a glance to Lina, "he said he would need to know how many times the lady was struck."

"Indeed, he would …"

"But there were relatively few spots on Raymond Dowdall's shirt and tie. If they hadn't been highlighted with a forensic marker, I would have missed them."

"Precisely!" said David Lean in the same tone that Archimedes must have uttered 'Eureka!' "The lady was struck seven or eight times. It was a ferocious attack and – as you've just realised – had Mr Dowdall been the attacker his shirt from would have been covered in blood."

"Why wasn't this brought up at the trial?"

"The Prosecution's case contradicted the forensic evidence. Our submissions were used to discredit Mr Dowdall's account and there was no reference to our full report in the judge's summing up."

"Because the circumstantial evidence surrounding Raymond Dowdall was sufficiently corroborated by the partial findings?"

"Yes. Our evidence was not questioned other than to give support to the Prosecution's case."

"And following my submissions to the Home Office for an appeal," said John Hayes, who spoke for the first time since the scientist arrived, "it was made quite clear that the forensic evidence 'was fully explored at the trial' – I remember the phrase, exactly – and that 'it was, of course, a matter for the jury to decide'."

"Twelve good men – women, too, these days – and true," said David Lean with a reluctant chuckle, "If I can be of further help, gentlemen, please do not hesitate to get in touch. I'll be only too happy to present my views as I would have been fourteen years ago."

David Lean collected his fedora and coat and left with it over his arm; for a moment the rain had ceased to fall.

"What do you make of him?" asked John Hayes, as soon as the door was closed.

"I suppose he was a junior fourteen years ago. Over-ruled."

"No doubt, but I wasn't impressed. He's sat on what he knew all this time."

"Like many others," replied Bingham, his tone expressing less than interest in what the newspaperman was saying, "PC Choudhury is going to question the three potential arsonists when they arrive, John. Perhaps you could keep in touch with her? I'm off to see another on Lauren Hagley's list and the Dowdall's list. One of those mentioned in those anonymous letters you received."

"Matthew Pretty?"

"Yes – the farmer."

"I've spoken with him on several occasions. His story changes every time. Likes a drink or three. I hope you find him sober. It's his wife who holds the farm together."

"Would you like to go with Bing, John?" suggested Lina, "I can stay in touch with PC Choudhury."

"Maybe not, Lina. I think Mr Pretty may have seen enough of me."

"Are you OK here, Lina?" asked Bingham.

"I'll be fine, Bing. Perhaps you'd drive me into Stoke, John, if you're going that way. I'll be on hand, then, and can do some shopping, but first I must ring Maureen Bassett to see how Phil is getting on. I'll make sure that he's contacted our solicitors, Bing, and if he hasn't, I'll see to it that Maureen makes him."

The farmyard was deep in mud after so many weeks of almost incessant rain and by the time he reached the house Bingham's shoes were covered in the dark brown soil, despite parking his car as closely as he could to the Pretty's front door. Despite her protests, he insisted that Mollie remained in their car; he had no wish to cope with a muddy dog along with his muddy shoes.

Mrs Pretty looked him up and down and smiled.

"We've been expecting you," she said, "Come in and take off those shoes. I'll clean them off while you and

Matt are talking. I'm used to this. Matt always wears leather boots – he can't abide wellingtons – and they're always covered in dirt. I don't suppose a coffee would go amiss. I'd offer you something stronger, only I want my husband sober. He's got work to do today. Hang it – no! I'll drop some rum in the coffee, or would you rather have a toddy. Christ, it's raw out there. The cold and the wet. Nothing worse. Come in and warm yourself. Matt! He's in the office."

"Why were you expecting me?" asked Bingham, once he'd removed his shoes and was sitting at the kitchen table.

"Reggie Morton phoned and said another nosey parker will be on his way. I'd heard you were around. I remember you from when you rounded up those gangsters …"

"It was the police who did that, Mrs Pretty. I played only a small part."

"That's not what the papers said, but then you can't believe all you read."

The farmer's wife hadn't stopped moving around the large kitchen as she spoke, and Bingham had watched her lips closely so he missed nothing she said, although her voice would have no doubt cut through his deafness.

She was a big woman but without an ounce of fat on her, the type described in old novels as 'peasant stock'. Bingham could imagine her shoeing a horse as readily as laying a table. She wore no makeup but her strong features needed none and still bore the attractiveness of her youth. Bingham placed her somewhere in her mid-forties, a woman by no means passed the peak of her desirability.

He looked quickly round the kitchen and it reminded him of his and Lina's, except it lacked the homeliness. It was a place to cook and eat, nothing more. Like the yard, it was functional but tidy, unlike many farmyards he'd seen in his time.

When she placed Bingham's toddy before him, alongside his coffee, she caught his eyes and held them; the look told Bingham that she was the one who made the decisions and had probably steered the courtship that brought about her marriage to Matthew Pretty.

"At last!" she said, as her husband appeared in the doorway that led from their sitting room. He was a stocky man with broad shoulders and thick hair. He reminded Bingham of a young Jack Nicholson and had the same devilish grin. 'One for the ladies', thought Bingham.

"All right, Meg, I just had to finish those returns."

"Go on through, Mr Bingham. I'll bring your drinks. You don't want to talk in the kitchen. I'll bring you a coffee, Matt."

As Bingham subsided into a soft armchair by a roaring log fire, he found himself thinking that this wasn't the welcome he'd envisaged. Accompanying him to his car, John Hayes had talked of Matthew Pretty 'evading all my attempts to see him' and hadn't mentioned Meg Pretty at all. It was probably nothing, not a thought on which to dwell, but Bingham set great store by the unexpected.

"Mr Pretty …"

"Matt – everyone calls me Matt."

"In that case, George. Matt, I'm not a police officer and not ruled by their constraints. I've no business being here and certainly no business asking you questions, and so ..."

"It's all right, George. I'm pleased to talk to you. You're not a newspaperman and you're not after a story; you're after justice, getting a young man out of prison who shouldn't have been put there in the first place."

"You believe Raymond Dowdall is innocent?"

"I've always believed that."

"It's true, George," said Meg Pretty, who'd obviously followed their conversation, as she placed a coffee and a toddy on a small table beside her husband, "Matt has always said that Raymond Dowdall wasn't the type."

"He was a quiet lad, a bit of a loner."

"What I'm trying to do, Matt, is place everyone where they were on that morning. Can you remember where you were?"

"I'm not likely to forget, George. That morning is printed on all our memories. I was at my mother's when it happened."

"What time was that?"

"Lunchtime. I used to go and see her at lunchtime once a week and that was the day. She passed on a few years ago."

"There's no chance you could have gone along the river path?"

"None at all."

"Not at any time that day?"

"No."

"What were you doing in the morning?"

"I had one or two suppliers to see in town."

"And in the afternoon?"

"I picked Matt up from his mother's," said Meg Pretty, "I needed the Land Rover that day. We only had the one vehicle."

"How did you get into town?"

"I dropped him off, of course."

"At what time?"

"It was early. I needed to get into Stoke."

"Where?"

"In the High Street. Does it matter exactly where?"

"Oh yes," said Bingham, "At least three witnesses place your husband near the river path. If they're wrong, we need to know why they seem so certain. There's no chance is there, Matt, that one of the people you visited was Reggie Morton?"

"I'm sure not."

"Not even for a drink?"

"No."

"And he didn't meet you anywhere?"

"No."

"Apart from your mother, who else did you see during the morning. You had several hours in hand."

"There was Walter Higgins – he was doing some work for us – and the seed merchant, and ..."

"You didn't see Raymond Dowdall?"

"No. I'm certain of that."

"When did you hear that Janet Bawley had been attacked?"

"It must have been while I was at my mother's, mustn't it?"

"How did your mother react when she heard the news."

"Well, she was shocked, of course."

"And sympathetic? Mrs Bawley had a reputation, didn't she?"

"I don't know what you mean."

"Your mother's generation had a word for women like Janet Bawley, didn't they? What did she say when she heard the news?"

"She was surprised … and shocked. My mother …"

"Who brought you the news?"

"I don't follow you."

"You were at your mother's for lunch and didn't leave until your wife picked you up. Someone must have brought you the news that Mrs Bawley had been attacked."

"Who was it, Matt? You must remember," said Meg Pretty.

"I think it was one of the workmen."

"Workmen?"

"There was work going on in the churchyard."

"Why would one of the workmen call at your mother's?"

"They knew I was there, I suppose."

"But why would they think you wished to know? Why would they trouble to come to your mother's house to find you?"

Bingham glanced up at Meg Pretty and saw the look in her eyes. At that moment, had she not been there, he was sure that Matthew Pretty would have thrown him out or got something off his chest. As it was, the farmer was in no position to make any move.

"Matt?" said his wife.

"Were you friendly with Janet Bawley before you met your wife?" suggested Bingham.

"We might have knocked around a bit – everybody did," replied Matthew Pretty, relief in both his voice and the look he gave Bingham.

"It's a small town, isn't it? Everybody knows somebody who knows you."

Matthew Pretty laughed; a laugh shot through with relief.

"That's certainly true," he said.

"I expect you both had quite a few admirers before you got together. How far away is the river path from where your mother lived?"

"It's the other side of the town," replied Meg Pretty, "Matt's mother lived on the Newton Road."

"The key to understanding why someone would want to murder Janet Bawley lies in understanding the relationships between her and those who knew her. She was considered to be what your mother might have called a loose woman. Is that not so? She kept a book grading the performances of the various men she saw as her conquests."

"You've seen this book?" asked Meg Pretty, with a hard laugh.

"Not yet, but I have the next best thing from two different people: a list of those men reputed to be Janet Bawley's lovers. Each of the names on those lists gave a statement to the police at the time, but we have now discovered that these statements were false. The police officers concerned did not exist."

"You mean someone, another police officer, was giving them false alibis?" suggested Meg Pretty.

"Yes."

"Who was the officer?"

"I must treat that knowledge as confidential, as I will treat what you tell me."

"It was Bill Charlton, wasn't it? He was the one who boasted that he'd broken the weird kid, got the confession out of him," said Meg Pretty, her voice full of contempt.

"Did you know Bill Charlton, Matt?" asked Bingham.

"Everyone knew Bill Charlton."

"How well? Were you drinking buddies?"

"We shared the occasional pint."

"Was it in the pub he boasted of having broken Raymond Dowdall?"

"It might have been."

"You'd remember, wouldn't you? Who else was there at the time?"

"It's a long time ago. I don't remember."

"Did you ever share a meal with him?"

"I don't think so."

"Yes, you did, Matt. You enjoyed that little restaurant in Stoke," said Meg Pretty.

"Oh yes."

"Was Reggie Morton with you at this restaurant?"

"He might have been."

"And Walter Higgins?"

"We held a business meeting there once or twice."

"And Gerald Osman? Am I right in thinking he may have met with you there?"

Matt Pretty had had enough. The farmer's fists clenched and unclenched, he reached for the toddy his wife had made and downed it in one swallow. Keeping his cool wasn't one of his characteristics but, at that moment, he had no choice. Bingham was well aware of the danger of a beating in which he might have stood. He looked at Meg Pretty, who once again gave him the impression that she was in charge.

"Reggie Morton and Gerald Osman were well-known to share a preference for a certain kind of woman, weren't they – *good sports*, ones who enjoy a *good slapping*? Would I be right? Did Janet Bawley fall into this category?"

"Who filled you with that rubbish?"

"Reggie Morton. Did he not tell you what we'd discussed during my visit when he phoned this morning?"

"Phoned?"

"Your wife said he phoned to warn you another nosey parker was on his way."

"You remember, Matt," cut in Meg Pretty.

"Yeah, yeah, I do now. I forgot."

"Did he also tell you that Walter Higgins, Martin Newham and a third man described as *a tougher character, big, muscled, looking for trouble* who refused to give his name were apprehended trying to burn down my home? The Suffolk police have preferred charges and they're now with your local force being questioned further. Did he mention that, Matt? I'm sure he did."

"Is this true, Mr Bingham?" asked Meg Pretty.

"Yes, Mrs Pretty. You see, the net is closing. Your husband is quite right to hold the conviction that Raymond Dowdall is innocent of the killing of Janet Bawley, but that means the actual killer has been at large for fourteen years. It's time he was trawled in."

"Do you know who it was?"

"Yes," said Bingham, "I do, and the man has a lot to answer for."

Chapter Eleven

HIS FACE PUFFY WITH TIREDNESS

Bingham was aware that Meg Pretty also had a lot to answer for: he had not planned for his interview with Matt Pretty to run as it did: only her presence had made that possible. He worked intuitively rather than deductively and set great store by the unexpected; Meg Pretty had been the unexpected.

When he arrived back at the White Hart, he was pleased that Lina had yet to return from the hospital and felt no need to venture there himself. His son would understand; Bingham knew that to be true. He was tired; the interview had worn him down and out. Sleep beckoned, and Bingham sat himself in the corner of the bar and dozed. He'd always been blessed with the catnap: twenty minutes and he'd be as right as rain, an image he found particularly inappropriate given the weather of the previous and current months, where rain had been anything but right. The young barmaid, the one who had gossiped to Martin Newham, placed a pint of Rev James on his table and left him to it.

When he woke, two hours later, Lina was watching him, sitting quietly with John Hayes, a smile on her face.

"You should have woken me," said Bingham.

"You weren't snoring."

"Mm!"

"How did you get on with Matthew Pretty, George?" asked John Hayes.

"He's rattled and I'm a little worried by the fact," replied Bingham and went on to describe the events at the farm and finished by asking the newspaperman, "So where does that leave us?"

"I think we have enough to approach Raymond's appeal lawyer, which I'd like to do just as soon as possible. I've given him a ring and he can see us this afternoon. Lina and I have been talking things over while you dozed, and we see the situation this way.

Dr Lean's evidence throws into question that put before the jury at the trial. PC Choudhury's discoveries regarding the unsigned statements indicate corruption at some stage during the early interviews. We believe that Mrs Bridge would come forward, as she was keen to do at the time, and testify that she saw Janet Bawley with another man – who she believes she could identify – not long before the killing must have taken place. We have learned that Walter Higgins was seen by a coachload of pensioners driving along Longshaw Lane on that very day, despite his assertions at the time that he was not in the village; many of the pensioners may be dead by now, of course, but the driver is likely to still be alive. The botched attempt to torch your house puts him and two others on the hot spot – if you'll excuse the image! – and we have the feeling that the Staffordshire police will get enough from them to warrant a re-opening of the case."

"It seems to me," said Lina, "that Mr Higgins may be the weak link in this chain of coercion. What he appears to have done on the day and since is typical of a man under pressure. I'd go as far as to say that at times he was unaware of what he was happening and his part in it. A basically decent man shackled by indecency."

"The lady you interviewed, George, Lauren Hagley, had a list of Janet Bawley's alleged lovers – men who were the subject of the false statements. I think the constabulary might be persuaded to interview them again," suggested John Hayes.

"What kind of man is this lawyer?" asked Bingham.

"An amicable young man in his twenties. His firm represents many of the inmates of Dovegate on routine matters such as prisoner complaints and parole applications. He's got his head screwed on. He warned me in the past that my involvement could actually harm Raymond's chances of parole, even spoil his chances of release. I took his meaning: it's not uncommon for prisoners who rock the boat to find their case taking a nosedive. The system doesn't like those who try to buck the system. He suggested that Raymond's file had been passed around like a hot potato for years, until someone found a dusty hole in which to lose it. Within the Home Office and the constabulary there is a firm belief that no one in prison is ever innocent.

He'll calm us down and put our 'evidence' into perspective. He'll see it through the eyes of the judiciary. You'll see what I mean when we meet him," said John Hayes, adding, when he sensed Bingham's hesitation, "You will come?"

It was something about Bingham's eyes that suggested otherwise, and Lina, knowing her husband like no one else ever could or would, said:

"You're thinking of going to see Janet Bawley's husband, aren't you, Bing?"

"I did wonder whether I should pay him a visit – and soon."

"He was reluctant to talk to me when we were trying to gather sufficient evidence to warrant our first appeal," said John Hayes, "I wanted his version of events. I felt a great deal of sympathy for him, but he wouldn't see me. He clearly thought of me as the man who was trying to defend his wife's killer."

"Understandably," said Lina.

Bingham said nothing, and Lina watched him drawing into himself; the glazed expression that came whenever he was deep in thought appeared in his eyes and manner. She'd noticed it at family gatherings such as birthdays and Christmases, and even when the two of them were deep in conversation. In the early days of their marriage, she'd been annoyed, thinking he'd lost interest in what she was saying; later, as she came to know him better, Lina realised that it signalled exactly the opposite.

Bingham was not looking forward to this meeting. He had telephoned Mark Bawley at the council offices in Stoke, where he had his office as a surveyor, and the man had, begrudgingly, agreed to speak with him that evening on the condition that "the newspapers aren't involved". When Bingham assured him that this was so, the murdered woman's widower had brought the meeting forward, and it was late afternoon when Bingham set out for the old farmhouse near Stone that the Bawleys had bought to renovate when they got back together.

In truth, Bingham was impressed by what he'd heard of Mark Bawley; he considered him a cut above the average man, and he didn't want to be disappointed by the reality when they met. Ever since Lauren Hagley told him of the man's attitude to his unfaithful wife and what he'd tried to do when they were reunited, Bingham had sensed that in many ways they were similar in character.

Lina had never been unfaithful to Bingham, but he knew that if ever this should happen, he would not hesitate to welcome her into his arms again. This wasn't a belief that he could formulate precisely in his mind: it was more of a feeling about love, and it was a feeling he knew he must share with this man he had never met; a man who in the eyes of the world had a greater motive for killing his wife than anyone else.

Mark would be a man in his mid-forties, perhaps slightly older. Had Bingham had children when most of his contemporaries did, in his twenties, his sons would now be the same age as Mark; and Bingham liked to think that his sons would be as magnanimous. It wasn't simply that he wanted his sons to be as he hoped himself to be but more that they would, by that age, have developed a view of other people that was based on a desire to understand rather than to judge.

Moreover, it was Mark Bawley's generation that Bingham had educated when he first went into teaching, and he needed to believe that those years had not been wasted. Whenever he met an ex-pupil or heard of what they were doing, Bingham crossed his fingers or touched wood and prayed that they were, whatever their shortcomings, compassionate adults.

He was aware that he knew nothing of Mark Bawley; except for the snippet he had garnered from Lauren Hagley, he was ignorant. The man had not been mentioned by anyone else, and yet, more than anyone else, he was at the centre of the events that led to his wife's death. Bingham had not clapped eyes on him; his appearance remained a mystery, the man a shadow.

Bingham was now going to find out if he was wrong: if he, an old man, was merely sentimental. He had prepared himself for this interview, not in any systematic way approved by the personnel manuals but through gathering his thoughts and feelings together into what he hoped was an informed intuition. He was, after all, not an official or a journalist; he had nothing to gain from this meeting other than ...

At that point, his thoughts stopped. He was going to see Mark Bawley because he was interested in him, but he knew there was more at stake than his own curiosity.

Driving through Stone, he almost stopped for a drink. He remembered a pub, the Royal Exchange, from his student days. It had been a classic English pub at that time, a really nice pub, where you could relax and feel welcome, with a friendly landlord and landlady who greeted you as though you were a regular and where the beer was well kept. As he passed it on his way through, Bingham resisted the temptation, not so much because he was concerned about drinking and driving, despite his concerns about the effect of alcohol on him now he was old, but more because he didn't want the smell of ale on his breath.

The farmhouse was certainly in a deserted area but had a comfortable appearance. The curtains were drawn, and a warm light glowed through them. In the porch, a light shone on the front door. The place had a clean, cared-for, appearance. Mark Bawley was waiting for him and opened the door before Bingham could use the iron knocker.

"Come in, Mr Bingham. I'll take your coat."

The lounge into which he was shown was lit by lamps and concealed bulbs, much to Bingham's relief: he had a dislike of bright, overhead lighting. Mark Bawley waved him into a large, leather armchair and offered him a drink. It was an agreeable room, snug, cosy; and Bingham was impressed that the man had also welcomed Mollie who now curled by Bingham's feet.

"Just a half of a low alcohol beer if you have one, please. I'm driving."

The widower left him only for a moment and returned with the drinks already poured from their bottles; Bingham noticed that his host had taken his other half into a large, German lager glass. Waste not, want not was his thought as Mark Bawley sat opposite to him and looked straight into his eyes.

"I've agreed to see you, Mr Bingham, because a colleague at work told me who you are and I remember having some admiration for what you did to apprehend those gangsters; but my stricture remains – nothing of what passes between us this evening finds its way to the newspapers. Is that understood?"

"Let me clarify two points. Firstly, my part in the apprehension of those gangsters was very small: the police did the spade work. Secondly, I am working with John Hayes on this investigation. He introduced himself to me and knows more about the case than I ever will; his help has been invaluable. This afternoon, he put our new evidence before Raymond Dowdall's appeal lawyer. That's something you need to accept, but nothing that is said between us tonight will go further – not even as far as my wife, if you insist on absolute confidentiality, and certainly not to the newspapers."

Bingham needed to assert his position and John Hayes's importance to the case; at the same time, he didn't want to stem the flow of any illumination Mark Bawley might cast on the case. The widower looked him over and seemed satisfied.

"You believe this Raymond Dowdall to be innocent?"

"Forensic evidence ignored at the trial suggests that it is almost impossible that he killed your wife. The blood splashings on him were minimal compared to those that he would have incurred had he beaten your wife almost to death with that branch."

Mark Bawley did not seem phased by Bingham's brutal explanation, which he delivered deliberately to test the other man's reaction. He wanted time to observe the surveyor, time to take him in. He was a small man, much shorter than Bingham had imagined, with soft facial features and a tenderness of expression that Bingham thought appropriate to a poet. This, he thought, confirmed the sensitive nature he'd expected of the man, and Bingham was pleased.

"The jury didn't think so at the time."

"As I said, evidence was ignored – possibly withheld."

"Why?"

"The forensic scientists disagreed and only the evidence that helped to establish Raymond Dowdall's guilt was submitted."

"But that's corruption!"

"Or simply a difference of opinion. The forensic team were not prepared to introduce conflicting views of what might have happened."

"That may well occur again. Do you have any other new evidence?"

"There are witness statements, giving alibis to men who might have been usefully questioned, unsigned, undated and written by police officers who didn't exist."

Mark Bawley's eyes widened. If Bingham was anything, he was succinct: at staff meetings during his working life, he would sum up an issue that others might spend hours discussing to no avail and no useful outcome. He thought he saw a smile sketch itself across the surveyor's face; this man, also a public servant subject to the waffle from Whitehall, was familiar with the value of brevity. It was important to Bingham that he gained Mark Bawley's confidence. He had come to alert the widower that any impending appeal would open up questions the other man might not want raised; but it was the very answers to those questions that Bingham needed.

"There were very few witnesses at the trial and none, as I remember, in Mr Dowdall's favour."

"They were frightened off, but guilt itself doesn't wear off – at least, not for people who have a conscience – and we have several potential witnesses who will now come forward."

"You're sure that's the case?"

"Yes. One who saw your wife with a man we must assume she had arranged to meet; at least one, and possibly several, who saw Walter Higgins in the town at the time he denies he was there; one who has a list of the names of the men with whom your wife appears to have associated; several ..."

"You're not one to pull your punches, are you, Mr Bingham?"

At that moment, Bingham was unsure what turn the conversation would take; it was a critical moment, and not one from which to flinch.

"A young man – little more than a boy at the time, has been in prison for fourteen years for a crime he did not commit. This isn't the time to pull punches."

Mark Bawley clearly possessed the ability to pullback from situations he found intolerable, to pigeon-hole them and get on with his life. He was a person of a scientific stamp, a man capable of an intelligent objectivity, an objectivity that showed the best way forward regardless of the feelings of the moment: his acceptance of his wife's infidelity was proof of that fact, and it was on this characteristic – an unusual one in his experience – that Bingham was relying.

"You mentioned Walter Higgins. I know Walter. He has done work for me on this house that Janet and I were renovating. He did work at the time. You're surely not suggesting that he and my wife were involved in any way?"

He was indignant, abashed by the thought that his wife might have found Walter Higgins desirable. It was, also, the first time that anyone had referred to the murdered woman solely by her Christian name; and it was instructive and touching that the person should be her husband.

"No," said Bingham, quickly, eager to keep their conversation on track, "I am not, but Mr Higgins was involved on the day your wife was murdered, just as he was involved two days ago in an attempt to burn down my home, together with two other men – Martin Newham and a thuggish type who refused to give his name but who we will identify now he's in the hands of the Staffordshire constabulary."

"They tried to burn down your house?"

"They claimed to be taking photographs of themselves pretending to do so but I don't think the police will buy that story. Martin Newham had already threatened me, and I shall testify to the fact."

"I didn't realise you'd been threatened, Mr Bingham."

"Not only me, Mr Bawley, but also my dog and, possibly, my son. Reggie Morton certainly arranged for one or the other – or both – to be run down."

Bingham's mention of another name, that of an Upton businessman, had a different effect on the widower. It wasn't so much the variance in their occupations that brought this change about, Bingham thought, but rather the type of man to whom his wife might have been attracted. Try as we might to bury the past, it comes to haunt us in our sleepless nights and Bingham supposed that Mark Bawley had experienced many of those; besides, the surveyor was clearly not a snob.

Mark Bawley remained quiet for a considerable time. He had been taken off-balance and needed time to recover his composure. For years, thought Bingham, this man has been playing a part, but was now facing himself and with courage. The surveyor had needed, ever since the brutal killing of his wife, to believe that he had done the right thing by her and her memory. He was now faced with reviewing his stance.

"I wasn't aware that there was the slightest doubt from the start," he said, eventually, easing himself into his speculations, "I was in no doubt and the police were in no doubt."

He looked at Bingham, possibly seeking agreement but Bingham was silent.

"The police went at length through the evidence. They were left in no doubt."

It was the third time he had used that word, and he looked at Bingham as he did so; both men were aware of its significance.

"I was aware of the rumours, of course," he said, looking desperately at Bingham for some sign of acknowledgement, "but the police were so sure. They were well up on the boy from the start. Bill Charlton came to see me. He told me all about him. He said they were waiting for him to do something so they could convict him. He'd made several attacks, but the police hadn't enough evidence to convict. I remember saying that it was a pity they couldn't have got him before he killed Janet."

Mark Bawley reached for his stein and took a long draught of the beer. It was the first time since they sat down that he'd touched the alcohol.

"Please, have your drink, Mr Bingham. I can't drink alone," he said, and there was an appeal in his voice.

Bingham took his half-pint glass and drained it off; the widower fetched more beer and poured him another glass. He, too, sensed their similarity; it was a relief to be drinking with a like-minded person. Despite the difference in their ages, they might have been old schoolfriends re-united after several years.

"I met Janet soon after I left university. I hadn't really had girlfriends before – at least, not in the way they do nowadays – and she knocked me off my feet. I'd bought a car, an MG, and she was impressed. We got engaged very quickly. Looking back, perhaps that was a mistake, but she seemed keen on the idea and her parents were pleased.

I've always worked for the council as a surveyor in Stoke. I love my job. It's part of my life. I wouldn't have it anyway else. My father used to say, 'a job worth doing is worth doing well', and I believe that's true. I often stayed late at work, and so Janet was left on her own a lot. It was selfish of me. I know that now. Janet loved socialising. Everyone liked her.

I'd heard rumours, of course, but I wasn't one to doubt my wife's word. She got caught up in the atmosphere of the town. Lots of her schoolfriends were married and they were a bad influence, and they had husbands who earned a sight more than me. I think they turned her head.

She was associating with people I didn't know, people who could swan around enjoying themselves all the while."

The county council surveyor reached again for his stein and drained it off. He looked at Bingham, whose recharged mug was still untouched, nodded with a smile and left for the kitchen, where he refilled his own glass and returned to his armchair. It was the first time Bingham had heard any bitterness in the man's tone, and he was sure that Mark Bawley was aware of the fact.

"I didn't feel these people were good for Janet. She was troubled in her own mind. I could see that for myself. I told her, quite forcefully, that I wasn't happy with the situation. I didn't think she was having affairs, but I did think her behaviour wasn't right for a married woman. I told her that if she wanted to do as she pleased, she would have to do it somewhere else ... I couldn't be certain that she wasn't having affairs, but I think I would have known."

He paused and took another long swig of his beer.

"Our marriage hit the rocks soon after, and Janet took lodgings elsewhere. We were apart for three years or more and then one day she got in touch and said she wanted to try and make a go of it again. I still loved her, despite everything – I always have – and so we tried to make a new start. It wasn't easy for either of us, but we tried. One problem was that we didn't have children. It might have kept her happier if we had – who knows? I think she was unfulfilled.

It was three years after we got back together that we moved here. It was to be our dream home. Janet was so enthusiastic about it ... The day it happened we'd been sitting together, here – in the kitchen. We had breakfast together. I remember kissing her goodbye when I went off to work ... It was the last I saw of her, conscious – the last time we spoke to each other.

The next thing I knew was when the police phone me at work. I dashed to the station at Longton and found myself in a cell and being interrogated, as though I was a criminal. I'd been at work until they phoned. How could I have killed Janet? They let me go the following morning and I rushed to the hospital with Janet's mother. Janet was still unconscious. We went back the next day and she died in the afternoon. She wasn't able to speak to us once."

Bingham had not taken his eyes off Mark Bawley since he began what in effect was a long confession, and he felt the man was trying to be sincere. He waited, still saying nothing to help the man before him; here was a someone coming to terms with the unpalatable.

"I still say she wasn't having these affairs – not after we got back together. I don't know why she was down by the river path that day but I'm sure it was for a good reason."

Was he so certain at the time? Could he have come forward with information that might have saved Raymond Downing his fourteen years' incarceration?

"After Janet's death, I had to go through her effects – that is the word, isn't it? I didn't want to; it was an intrusive act … I came across this."

Mark Bawley left the room and made for the stairs that led from the corner of the room. When he returned, his face puffy with tiredness, he held a little black book in his hand.

"I locked it away in a drawer, one of the drawers of her dressing table. It was obviously a personal item, like a diary, because it was wrapped around with a pink ribbon. I didn't look at it then and I haven't looked at it since."

Chapter Twelve

HOW QUIET ... FOR SO LONG

For the second night running, Bingham was sitting by the window, rain still pouring across the panes, when Lina woke in the early hours, having sensed that he was no longer in the bed with her. She rose quietly, made him a cup of tea and placed it in his hands without speaking. She had no need to ask him what he was thinking because she knew: the same thoughts were running through her own mind.

For years, Mark Bawley had lived what amounted to a lie; if not a precise untruth, then a deception that allowed him to live with the actual truth. He was a quiet man, no doubt a man who loved his home and his wife. It was enough for him that he did a good, probably excellent, job and that he could return each night to a warm, loving home, a home shared by someone of a similar mind. He was a provider, pleased to provide.

He was respected at work and took pleasure in the acknowledgements of his colleagues. To achieve that status in the public sector he had also to be single-minded, very clear about why he had chosen his profession and how he went about his craft. He was a satisfied man, satisfied by his achievements and what these had made possible.

He had met and married Janet quite soon after leaving university. He would have approached the idea of marriage with the same single-mindedness he applied to his work, thought Lina. Love had driven him, and he probably gave little thought to how his future wife might view marriage and what her needs might be. His experience of women before her might have amounted to very little. His appreciation of what his wife needed from life would have been unrealistic, his understanding marred by inexperience.

'Her enthusiasm came in phases' was the phrase used by Lauren Hagley to describe her friend. How had Mark coped with such a personality?

He seemed to love her enough to accept that she might have formed associations with other people, associations he considered unacceptable but not associations that involved sexual infidelity. Was that how he rationalised his feelings how he accepted the situation because he needed peace at home?

There was much to be said for home: comfort, a meal on the table, a light in the window, someone to draw the curtains on a dark night, conversation around the fireside or the television. The contentment he had lost when his wife left him returned with her when she asked to come back; and he was satisfied with the arrangement.

From what had been said, there seemed to have been no anger in the marriage, no bitterness. In significant respects their lives had been led separately and yet they remained together, husband and wife, each happy in their own way. Mark Bawley had built up his world around him and done all he could to hold it together.

After her death he had gone through her effects because that was the proper thing to do and he had come across her little, black book. He hadn't looked at it because that would have destroyed the illusion he held of their marriage; instead, he had locked it away in a drawer, content with not knowing.

He had accepted the explanations of the police that they had convicted the right person for a similar reason, despite the unlikelihood that a seventeen-year-old boy with no apparent motive had committed such an atrocity.

He wouldn't have slept after Bing left. He would have felt obliged at last, fourteen years later, to open the little, black book tied with the pink ribbon. Still striving not to believe what he read, Mark Bawley would have seen his wife with the men whose sexual performances she rated on a scale of one to five. He knew the men. He had seen them, spoken with them, while his wife was alive; he had passed the time of day with them since her death.

He had offered Bingham a drink, but Lina felt, judging by the way her husband described Mark Bawley's drinking, that he did so only in company: he had filled his glass twice in a short time and swallowed the contents without enjoyment.

And Bing had pulled no punches. Could he have acted otherwise? A young man had been incarcerated for almost half his life while the real killer was still on the loose. The Home Office had shown no interest in the evidence presented by John Hayes at two previous appeals. Was there any guarantee they would do so now?

Lina moved away from the window, as the thought crossed her mind. Why had her husband gone to see

Mark Bawley? She had known he was going without his having to say so, and she'd assumed it was out of sympathy, arising from a desire to warn the man that disclosures that would distress him were likely to become public. She made a second cup of tea with the two remaining tea bags and brought it to him. Bingham had still not moved and accepted the hot drink with a smile but without a word.

He had forced Mark Bawley to face the truth about his wife, a truth the man did not want to acknowledge, a truth he had kept from himself for so long. What would he do now? Had he, like Bing, realised who the killer might be? Her husband hadn't said much on his return; he'd conveyed to her Mark Bawley's 'confession' in detail but offered no information as to what he'd said himself, if anything.

The rain driving at the window made Lina shiver. She looked at the sky; there would be no sun that day, nothing but endless clouds flooding the earth with rain. Cold and dreary: a day for wrapping up well if you went out or, better still, sitting by the fire with toasted crumpets. Lina couldn't see that happening.

The knock on the door woke them both, cuddled as they were in each other's arms for warmth. They'd returned to bed and as so often happens when you wake in the early hours they had slept late.

"Mr Bingham, there's a phone call for you!"

The voice of the lady who came to prepare breakfast for the guests sounded anxious. Bingham slipped, or rather fell, from the bed and pulled on his dressing gown.

"It's the phone on the bar, Mr Bingham."

The woman smelled of fried bacon and sausages. Some guests must already be at breakfast, thought Bingham, as he hurried down the stairs and made his way, apologising for his appearance, to the bar.

"Mr Bingham, it's Meg Pretty. Mark Bawley has been here. He's just left with Matt's shotgun."

"I take it you're OK?"

"You could say that. Can you come over?"

"Of course. I'll be right there."

"Do get dressed first. They told me you were still in bed."

Bingham imagined the smile on the strong face as she spoke, but her tone was anxious. While he dressed hurriedly, an obligation he disliked intensely, Bingham brought Lina up-to-date and asked her to phone both the police and John Hayes.

"Don't forget your phone, Bing: we need to keep in touch. I charged it last night."

Bingham smiled his thanks, a wry smile since he accepted the reproof, kissed his wife goodbye and made his way downstairs and out to the small yard at the back of the pub where his car was parked, a cry from the woman who came to prepare breakfast, a meal he would now forego, ringing in his ears.

The incessant rain overnight had reduced the already muddy farmyard to little more than a swamp. Bingham backed his car up almost to the door and hurried in, telling Mollie to stay put. She wasn't happy about the order, but he couldn't face a muddy dog at that moment.

Meg Pretty held the door open for him and the first thing he noticed was the bruising on her face, around the left eye and cheek.

"It was Matt," she said, "It's the first time ever and it will be the last."

"I'm sorry," replied Bingham.

"No need for you to be. Someone had to broker the truth. Come in, I expect you missed breakfast, didn't you? Let me get you some."

"There's no need."

"There's every need. If I'm not mistaken, you've a busy day ahead. I'll tell you what happened while I cook."

"Just an egg on toast, then, please," said Bingham."

"How do you like your eggs?"

Bingham laughed – he could barely believe the conversation they were having – and Meg Pretty responded likewise.

"An army marches on its stomach, Mr Bingham."

Meg Pretty's sentiment was true. Someone's triangle (Bingham couldn't quite remember who's, but it would come to him in the small hours) placed food at the base: food, clothing, shelter – the essential bases for living.

"After you'd gone yesterday, I had it out with Matt and he didn't like it. His lie about a workman coming to his mother's house to give him the news was too insulting to be ignored. Matt has his good points and we've had our good times but I'm not being treated like an idiot in front of someone else."

"How long had you known?"

Meg Petty looked at Bingham, a hard look, a not-too-friendly look, as though he'd peeped inside her mind and invaded her privacy.

"From the beginning, I suppose. A wife knows; but I'd sat on it, as one does. But after what you made him say, I couldn't sit on it any longer. He had to be honest with me. I needed to know it all – the lies about the meetings in the restaurant in Stoke and the phone call from Reggie Morton, and the rest ... I needed it all cleared up."

She placed a plate of food in front of Bingham – three fried eggs on an equivalent number of rounds of toast, the largest breakfast Bingham had eaten for a decade – together with a scalding cup of tea, and sat opposite to him, across the kitchen table, hands clasped around her own mug.

"Did you suspect he might have been involved in the murder?"

It was the question she'd been waiting for, the one that needed answering.

"Not until yesterday but then I knew. He's never been a violent man – rough yes, but never violent. He's never raised his fist against me – not until last night. I pushed him hard. I had to know the whole truth.

After our row, after he'd hit me, he cleared off. He was ashamed, but he needn't worry. He'll not get the chance to be ashamed again."

"Do you know where he went?"

"He'll have found some of his drinking buddies. He'll be in a right state this morning, drinking all night."

"Where would they be drinking?"

"There's one they like at Denstone, another at Ellastone. It's hard to tell. They may be at one of his mate's houses. Some of the wives don't care. I'll write you list. I said you'd a busy day ahead."

Had Pretty any reason to suppose that Mark Bawley would be looking for him? It seemed unlikely: he was unaware that Bingham had even spoken to the murdered woman's husband.

"What did you tell Mark Bawley?"

"Much the same as I've told you."

"Why?"

"Why not."

The answer sounded evasive, and Bingham wondered what had passed between the two, one the wife of a man she might well believe to be a killer, the other the husband of the suspected killer's victim. Seeing Meg Pretty for the independent spirit she was, he thought they might have a good deal in common.

"What happened when Mark Bawley got here?"

"He asked to see Matt."

"Did he have anything with him?"

"Such as?"

"A weapon of any kind."

"Not when he arrived."

Bingham's patience, much as he liked Meg Pretty, was wearing thin. He polished off his breakfast, leaving his plate wiped clean with the third round of toast, and downed the tea before he addressed the woman again, and then it was with a look rather than words.

"He was very polite," said Meg Pretty, a note of resignation in her voice, "He knocked on the door, asked for Matt and waited to be invited in. When I told him Matt had gone out last night and not returned, he asked if he could look round. I laughed. I don't think anyone has doubted my word before. I suppose he thought I was protecting Matt. He came in and had a look in all the downstairs rooms, and I asked him if he wanted to go upstairs. He didn't find it funny. I think it was then he noticed the bruising on my face. He didn't say anything, but I could see he was upset. As I said, he was very quiet."

"Too quiet?"

"Yes, Mr Bingham, too quiet. He was a man with a purpose, if you see what I mean. You could tell that there was just one thing on his mind, and that was to find Matt and have it out with him."

"But you still told him where your husband might be?"

"I gave him the name of the pubs."

"But not the addresses of the friends?"

"No."

"Write them all down for me, will you? Not Gerald Osman or Reggie Morton or Walter Higgins – those I know – but any others where your husband might have gone."

Meg Pretty opened one of the drawers of the kitchen table and brought out a notepad and pen. Once again, as on his first visit, Bingham was reminded of their kitchen at home. Lina had such drawers and in them, among letters and cards from family and friends, she kept her wiring materials: notepad, envelopes, stamps and an assortment of pens; but, once again, he was reminded of how the atmosphere of each place differed. If buildings spoke of love, one kitchen did rather more so than the other.

"Why is it that I know you'll find him, Mr Bingham?" said meg Pretty as she handed over the list of names and places.

"I've no idea, Mrs Pretty."

"Please call me Meg, when we meet again."

"George," he replied.

She was silent and Bingham was about to get up and leave when he realised she had something else to say. Their glances locked and he waited.

"When Mark Bawley was here, he saw Matt's gun propped up behind the kitchen door. He took it with him."

"It was loaded?"

"Matt's not particular. I imagine so."

"May I use your phone?"

"It's on the wall."

Bingham made three calls: one to Lina, one to John Hayes and the other to Staffordshire constabulary before joining Mollie in his car and driving off to Gerald Osman's rundown house by the quarry.

John Hayes on receiving Lina's call had driven straight to the Rambler's Rest and Reggie Morton, not so much as to warn Morton but to protect Mark Bawley.

John Hayes had never liked the hotelier. During the years he had struggled to find evidence that might throw into doubt the likelihood that Raymond Dowdall was the killer, he had found Reggie Morton to be nothing more than an obstreperous bully, a man safe in the knowledge that if things got too hot for him a good thumping from some of his friends would soon sort out those causing him hassle.

The news that it was almost certain he had arranged – and how quickly! – to have George Bingham's dog run over had only confirmed the newspaperman's in-built dislike.

He objected, also, to women being treated with anything but respect. No doubt there were those who enjoyed a 'good slapping' and considered the Reggie

Morton's and Gerald Osman's of this world to be 'real men'; but that wasn't John Hayes's world and those two were not his kind of men.

With the attempted arson attack on George and Lina Bingham's home, matters had come to a head, and John Hayes hoped that soon the police force would be rounding up the usual suspects for a bit of a grilling. He smiled as the phrase from his favourite film crossed his mind, despite its foolishness because the suspects in this case – the Janet Bawley Murder Case: he could visualise the headlines – were anything but 'usual'.

It was still early when he arrived at the walkers' hotel and staff were waking to the day. He was informed that "Mr Morton was unavailable" to which he had the joy of replying that "Mr Morton might prefer to be available rather than face a good thrashing". The girl at reception frowned, muttered something about "zero tolerance towards the abuse of staff" and shuffled off to find her boss who suffered zero tolerance to anything or anyone he felt might offer a threat to him.

"You?" he said when he appeared from the door behind the reception desk, but John Hayes noticed that he looked daunted if not dishevelled and there was a look of concern lurking somewhere in the back of his eyes.

"We need a chat."

"Come in," replied the hotelier, without hesitation, and ushered the retired newspaperman into his private quarters that John decided served as a boudoir as well as an office, judging by the couch.

The two men, adversaries for so long, looked at each other without speaking. John was undecided as to whether he should first alarm the fat man that the truth was on its way or warn him that he might be facing the husband of the woman for whom he had shown such little regard over the years. He preferred the former but for Mark Bawley's sake decided on the latter.

"You ought to know," he said, "that Janet Bawley's husband may well pay you a visit."

"He already has," replied Reggie Morton, smiling at the fact that he was at least several steps ahead of the journalist, "I sent him packing with the police on his heels. No one threatens Reggie Morton with a gun and gets away with it. You need to choose your company more carefully, Mr Hayes."

"He walked in here with a gun?"

"I didn't say that. Be careful how you quote me."

"What makes you think he had a gun?" asked the journalist who had yet to receive Bingham's call.

"He told me he had. Said he'd picked it up at Matt's farm."

John Hayes was taken off kilter. He and Bingham were concerned with protecting the murdered woman's husband; they didn't want him injured by these men or deflecting the police and public's attention from the evidence they had gathered. They both believed, following Meg Pretty's call, that Mark Bawley was attempting to find his wife's killer; neither had any idea his might be a mission of revenge.

"Do you know where he's gone?"

"Somewhere the police will find him."

"That's no answer."

"What reason have I to give you one?"

"Because none of us wants another killing. Where did you send Mark Bawley?"

"I don't know where he went. He'd already been to the farm. I suggested he might ask Walter Higgins who's been released, I understand, or have a chat with some of Matt's friends in Denstone or Ellastone," and added, with a laugh, "I said they might be able to help."

"And when he left you phoned the police?"

"Too true. We can't have people running around with guns, can we? You didn't know about the gun, did you?"

"No, no, I didn't."

"The thing about you newspapermen is that you're so keen to get a good story you don't always check the facts."

His mocking tone annoyed John Hayes, but the journalist could see that the hotelier was also nervous, brazen but frightened, unsure where recent events, so unusually out of his control, might lead.

"Where in Denstone and Ellaston?" he asked.

"You don't need to know that, Mr Hayes."

"The police will."

"The police will go where I tell them. I can give them the names of a couple of pubs to keep them busy."

"You've phoned Matt Pretty, haven't you?"

"He'll be waiting for Mr Bawley with a few friends. It doesn't pay to cross us, Mr Hayes: friends look after themselves."

Realising he could gain nothing more by staying, he was deciding to phone Bingham when his mobile rang, and he heard Bingham's voice on the other end of the line.

PC Mehreen Choudhury was on duty when Reggie Morton's call arrived at the station in Stoke-on-Trent, and that pleased her. Bingham had been right to wonder whether he was being helped or tailed; but to be fair it was mixture of both.

The station at Longton had a new broom and one that liked to sweep clean: a young man who'd only recently seen thirty but had all the qualifications needed and had been fast-tracked in the belief that success in any public sector organisation came from the top and had little to do with the experience of those at the coal face or with those who did the footwork. Not that this was true of Chief Inspector Dale Wright; he was a product of his time but one that had respect for his men and women, especially PC Choudhury, who he saw as a fast-track contender herself.

He'd wondered, since his arrival, about the Bawley Case and when Busybody Bingham had appeared on the scene, he saw his chance to do a bit of sweeping clean without having been seen to pick up the broom himself. He didn't like the idea that the force should bare stains of any kind; after all, a clean town reflected well on those appointed to keep it clean. He had come across the discrepancies PC Choudhury brought to Bingham's attention, having read thoroughly through the paperwork, They seemed to point, in the main, to one officer and a retired one, which was a distinct advantage when bringing corruption into the light of day.

When Lina Bingham's call arrived, he called Mehreen Choudhury immediately. She had no personal ambitions herself. She wanted to do well in the force but had no burning desire to 'get on', as the expression goes. She wanted to be an excellent 'copper' (she liked the old word) but more than that she wanted to fall in love, marry the right man and raise a large, loving family.

Mehreen liked the new boss's office. It had been newly furnished when he arrived and he kept it looking that way: clear carpet, clear desk, clear chairs, clutter free, unlike his predecessor. The boss worked late when on duty; 'never leave to tomorrow what you can do today' was clearly his motto, and he lived up to it.

"Things are on the move, Mehreen," he said in carefully modulated tones, "We've just had a call from Mrs Bingham, who tells us that Mr Bawley is looking for Mr Pretty and that her husband has gone to the Pretty's farm. I think we've reason enough to be concerned and take a few precautionary steps. We'll send cars to Mr Morton's, Mr Osman's and Mr Pretty's – and to Mr Higgins, who was released this morning – just to ensure their safety.

Intelligence is the key these days, Mehreen – thinking ahead, outside the box. Better to prevent a crime than to have to clear up the mess afterwards. And with what Mr Higgins has told us, I think we might be within our rights to ask some of these gentlemen in for questioning."

When Mehreen left to make the necessary arrangements, Chief Inspector Wright leaned back in his chair. He was the picture of modernity: fit, healthy, neat in appearance, a man with a ready smile for everyone and for himself, and this morning he had reason to smile: intelligence (the modern word for information as distinct from its original meaning: an ability to think analytically) had put him in a position to anticipate and prevent what could amount to a number of unseemly brawls on his patch.

What he didn't know as he sat contented with the morning's work was that Mark Pretty had a shotgun, something that Mehreen Choudhury was soon to discover when she arrived at the Rambler's Rest.

When Bingham arrived at Gerald Osman's, the police had already been and gone, leaving one officer on duty as a precautionary measure. The young officer was loath to allow Bingham into the house, until Chief Inspector Wright assured him that "busybody though he is, Mr Bingham can be trusted'; trusted, he hoped without expressing the thought, to upset the apple cart.

Gerald Osman was slumped in his chair by the fire, which had died on him. The fit, sprightly man from whom Bingham had struggled to gain information was a sorry sight, his air of distinction gone. The room that Bingham had noticed as tidy seemed to share its owner's dejection and Bingham didn't bother to ask permission for Mollie to sit with him across the fireplace.

Gerald Osman looked at him, said nothing but gave Bingham a glare that implied in no uncertain terms that he should have kept his nose out of things.

"Has Mark Bawley been here?"

"You know he has."

"Where did he go?"

"How should I know?"

"Because he must have left before the police arrived and you would have told him where to go."

"I don't want any trouble, Mr Bingham."

"You said that when we spoke last time, Mr Osman, but if you're in the habit of boasting that you 'finished the bitch off' trouble's likely to come your way. Where did you send Mark Bawley?"

"Who told you I said that?"

"Didn't you?"

"It was the drink – nothing more. Do the police know this?"

"If they don't, they soon will. Whoever told me will tell them."

Bingham couldn't remember, for the moment, who had told him. His memory wasn't what it was, but he thought it must have been John Hayes. Who had told John Hayes? He recalled something about a man at a bar who had listened to Reggie Morton boasting.

"Your friend, Reggie Morton, has boasted that the real killer will never be caught because he's too clever. Is that right?"

"How should I know?"

"You keep using that phrase, Mr Osman. How do you think it will stand up to police questioning? Those people are trained. They know what they're doing. We've spoken with your 'friendly copper'."

"Who?"

"There you go again. You'll be denying next that you and Reggie Morton prowl the motorways looking for a bit of slap and tickle – especially the slap. Did you or he ever give Janet Bawley a good slap?"

Gerald Osman looked up at Bingham, slumped and now shaken he wondered what the other man knew. Had Reggie Morton talked? What had Walter Higgins had to say that would land them in it? He'd had nothing to do with it. He was sure of that but were the police and this the bloke sitting opposite him? He'd had enough prison in his lifetime and he wasn't going down for someone else.

Bingham read it all in the man's face. 'Least said, soonest mended' wasn't an aphorism appropriate to the moment.

"Matt was here," he said, "I sent him on his way."

"This was last night, after he'd knocked his wife around?"

"He hit Meg?"

"What did he want?"

"Company. You'd upset him something bad. You'd have been better keeping out ..."

"Never mind the slogans," snapped Bingham, "Where did Pretty go?"

"Where he always goes. He's got mates up near Denstone."

"Did you go with him?"

"No. He wasn't pleased, but I'd had enough, although I didn't know he'd hit Meg."

"What difference would that have made?"

"Nothing, nothing."

"What were his plans?"

"How should I ..."

"Don't start that again! Was it just company he needed or was he up to something, since he wanted you with him?"

"He didn't know about Bawley. He was worried about what the police might have got out of Higgins and the kid. He thought we might need to take measures."

"You didn't tell the police this, of course?"

"What do you think?" replied Gerald Osman with a laugh.

"So, what did you tell them?"

"I gave them the names of a few pubs where they might find Matt."

"This morning?"

"I said he might have slept it off. Some of the pubs round here are 'open' all night – if you get what I mean and are a regular. The cops know that."

"But they won't find Pretty at any of them?"

"No."

Bingham felt he was pumping the handle of a dry well. He needed to be on the move. John Hayes had told him that Reggie Morton had sent the police on a wild goose chase also, but that Mark Bawley was on his way to meet Pretty and his friends. He was anxious now: time was running out if they were to avoid a catastrophe.

"I need to know where Mr Pretty is, Osman. Mark Bawley is on his way his way to find him."

"I know. He was here before the cops arrived."

"And you told him?"

"Where Matt is. We keep in touch, Mr Bingham. No one runs rings round us."

"Mark Bawley has a gun – Pretty's shotgun."

"I know. He showed me."

"He threatened you?"

"No. You might say he was ice cool. In fact, I've never seen anyone cooler. Icy he was – you know, Mr Cool."

"It never occurred to you that you might be the one he was after?"

"At first, and I'm not sure he wouldn't have come back later, but he won't now."

Bingham had often been struck forcibly by what he considered unbelievable – the simple truth that so many people were only able to see situations from their own point of view. Both Reggie Morton and Gerald Osman had been frightened by Mark Bawley: John Hayes had told him of the 'daunted' appearance of the hotelier and he had seen for himself how fear had slumped Osman in his chair; and yet both had become cocky once their immediate danger was over. They'd assumed what they supposed was their public persona.

Neither of them had seen the situation from Mark Bawley's viewpoint; neither of them had made any attempt to understand what was going through the mind of the murdered woman's husband. Mark Bawley had learned and, more importantly, come to accept, in less than twenty-four hours that his wife had carried on with a variety of men who had then conspired in one way or another to kill her; moreover, he had sat on his own wilful ignorance to such an extent that a boy had spent fourteen years in prison, and Mark Bawley was a man with a conscience, no matter how quiet it had been for so long.

Mark Bawley was now a man with one fixed idea: how he might put matters right. He was also a man subdued by humiliation, the humiliation brought about by three of the men he had visited that morning, one of whom had battered his wife almost to death with the branch of a tree.

Chapter Thirteen
A VAGUE GESTURE IN REPLY

Following her call to Mehreen Choudhury, who told her that Walter Higgins had been charged and released on bail pending his trial, Lina Bingham hurried, but cautiously, along the wet and slippery streets of Upton to the Higgins's house. She had become aware as she approached seventy that one slip might result in an ankle remaining broken for many months, an ankle that might never fully recover; wounds in the old take a long time to heal.

As it was, she made it easily and quickly, and Milly Higgins was more than pleased to open her front door and see Lina smiling on the doorstep.

"I thought you'd appreciate a little company, Milly. This must be very stressful for you."

"They tell me it was your house, Mrs Bingham," said the woman, her voice querulous.

"Never mind that. No harm was done. And you must call me Lina."

"Wally's not arrived yet."

"No, but it won't be long."

"Do you think he'll go to prison, Mrs Bingham?"

"I don't know to be honest, Milly. We'll have to see. There's no point rushing into things."

The common phrases were reassuring, and Milly Higgins smiled.

"It's so embarrassing. I thought we'd done with all this."

"It's best for the truth to come out, Milly."

"Yes, but the truth for who?"

While they were speaking, Milly had guided Lina into her living room where, once again, she took a long look at the photographs on the sideboard, while Milly made the inevitable cup of tea and brought it through with a digestive biscuit. The atmosphere was friendlier than on Lina's previous visit and they talked amicably and easily, considering the circumstances, until there was a knock on the door and Walter Higgins returned home, shame-faced and contrite.

"What have you done? What shame have you brought on us, Wally?"

"I know. Don't go on. Let me get in first."

It did go on, his account of the ill-fated expedition to Suffolk; it went on and on, and around in circles and was in its third phase of contrition when John Hayes arrived. He gave Lina a hug and sat next to her on the settee, accepted Milly's offer of a cup of tea and sat facing Walter Higgins so that the handyman had no choice but to meet his gaze. A look from Lina told him what had transpired but the journalist was in no mood to be conciliatory.

"I'm here because George and I thought you might be in some kind of trouble from these erstwhile friends of yours. The police are also likely to be sending an officer over to keep an eye on things. Mark Bawley has gone after – well, who knows! He's been to see your friend, Reggie Morton …"

"No friend of mine."

"Friend enough to do his dirty work, Walter! There's a good chance, he's also been to see Gerald Osman. Your husband's there, now, Lina. He's making his rounds is Mark Bawley – and he's armed."

"You don't think he'll come after my Wally?"

"I should think that very unlikely, Mrs Higgins. Your Wally – and it's a suitable name for him – is in more danger from his friends than his enemies. Isn't that right, Walter?"

"I've told the police all I know."

"Did they get around to your part in the murder of Janet Bawley?"

"Steady, John," said Lina, reaching across and placing her left hand firmly on his arm.

"The time for 'steady' is over, isn't it, Walter?"

"Leave me in peace. I'm saying nothing more now."

"I never knew you were involved in that, Wally. I thought you said you weren't in the village that day. Oh, my word, what terrible things we have to face."

The poor woman sobbed, and Lina crossed to where she sat (her habitual chair by the fireside for so many years) and placed her arms around the stricken woman. All four sat in silence while her tears fell and until they dried, streaked across her face. Whatever happened now, life would never be the same again.

"Tell me all, Wally. I must know. I've been a good wife to you. I deserve the truth."

"I can't. I got dragged into things I had nothing to do with. I'm not perfect, but I'm not the kind of man they're making me out to be."

"Shall I tell your wife what happened, Walter," said John Hayes, and it wasn't a question.

The handyman looked up at the journalist, aware that this was the man who for years had pursued the truth only to meet threats, hostility and a vicious wall of silence from those local people who might have had the courage and decency to come forward and help him. He nodded and looked down at his feet.

"Raymond Dowdall said from the beginning that he'd seen your husband's van at the crossroads on that day, but since nobody else had – not his employer, Mr Roberts, or the police who attended the scene of the crime – Raymond's account was ignored. It's true, that later some pensioners on a coach trip said they'd seen your husband driving along Longshaw Lane, but this sighting wasn't followed up because the police believed they'd got their man – or rather, boy. But Walter's van was there with a purpose, wasn't it?"

The handyman kept his eyes on his feet, avoiding all eyes, his wife's, in particular.

"Walter had been at Reggie Morton's hotel …"

"You told me you were out of the village, Wally."

"I was. It was the truth. I was up at Oakamoor doing a job for Harry Cotton when Reggie called me mid-morning. He had a problem with some guttering he wanted me to see to right away. You know Reggie. So, I sorted things out with Harry, told him I'd be back in no time and hurried to the Rambler's."

"Was it true?"

"The guttering? There was a bit loose. It could have waited but he didn't want it falling on any guests. So, I got to it."

"And you were there when the call came through at 12.15 – or thereabouts?"

"Yes."

"Reggie Morton received a call from a friend of his," continued John Hayes, "The friend was in trouble. He'd just killed a girlfriend – or thought he had – and needed to get away from the scene of his crime quickly. And so, Reggie obliged by sending Walter along with his van ..."

"I didn't know. I'd no idea. He just said he needed me to pick a friend up at the crossroads. It wasn't 'til I saw him – covered in blood he was – that I knew something was wrong. It was too late, then. He climbed into the back off my van and told me to get away fast. What could I do?"

"Wally, you knew what you could do," said Milly Higgins, "Who was it?"

"A young woman, searching for her dog, came across a couple in the copse," continued John Hayes, remorselessly, "She didn't know who they were at the time but later realised it was Janet Bawley when she saw her picture in the paper. She didn't know the man either but described him as stocky with broad shoulders and thick hair. She also said he was wearing workman's boots covered in dirt. This would have been sometime between noon and 12.15. Her evidence was dismissed at the first appeal hearing because she hadn't come forward at the time ..."

"Why didn't she and save us all this trouble?" asked Milly Higgins.

"Tell your wife, Walter."

"She'd have been scared."

"Exactly! Fear has stalked this case from the very beginning – the fear of retribution. Isn't that right, Walter?"

The handyman nodded.

"It was the main reason your husband was persuaded to set fire to Mrs Bingham's home ..."

"We never intended ..."

"So, you said. We'll let the courts decide. Where did you take the killer, Walter?"

"To a friend's place. He got cleaned up and borrowed some fresh clothes."

"And you burnt his own?"

"Yes."

"We knew none of this six days ago," continued John Hayes, "but once we'd accepted that Raymond Dowdall's account was accurate, it was a matter of filling in the details. As your husband said, Lina, 'everything was in place at that moment, in those fifteen minutes, if only we had recognised it, if only the police had recognised it at the time'.

Why was your husband where he said he wasn't? Who had Janet Bawley arranged to meet that day? The young woman's description didn't fit Walter Higgins or Reggie Morton or Gerald Osman ..."

"Pretty!" said Milly Higgins, "Matthew Pretty. Oh Wally, what have you done?"

When they left the Higgins's house, acknowledging the young policeman who nodded to them from his squad car, Lina said to John Hayes:

"Was it planned? Did Reggie Morton know what Matthew Pretty intended to do, and have Walter Higgins on hand?"

"That's a matter for the police to discover and the courts to decide, Lina."

"Where's Bing?"

"On his way to Pretty's friend's house, as far as I know."

"I've had enough if this, John. I expect you have, too."

John Hayes supposed correctly: Bingham had plucked the addresses of Matthew Pretty's friends from Gerald Osman: the slapper of women had decided it best to let Bingham know rather than face a visit to the police station where he would face a battery of questions based on what Bingham and John Hayes had discovered. Bingham immediately phoned Mehreen Choudhury.

"You have done the right thing, Mr Bingham. Now stay clear and leave this to us."

Bingham did not reply. Although Mark Bawley had a shotgun, Bingham didn't consider himself in personal danger, and it seemed important to try to reach him before armed officers did so. It wasn't like the old days when a local bobby, known to someone like Mark Bawley, would talk him down; nowadays, from what Bingham had seen on television, officers went in with guns at the ready. You couldn't blame them – terrorism, thuggery and armed villains were on the increase in Britain – but he didn't want to see Mark Bawley shot dead.

Osman had given him two addresses, the first accessed by a series of lanes. He entered a rain drenched Ellastone on the B5032, passed the Duncombe Arms and headed northwest. Several twists and turns later, along winding one-track lanes, he came to a pair of cottages, originally no doubt the homes of farm labourer's but now knocked into one. The fencing was new, the garden immaculate and so the slatternly woman who opened the door was a surprise to Bingham. The fag in her mouth, drooping over a lip adorned with yesterday's makeup, did nothing to improve her image; she stared at Bingham aggressively and he was in no doubt that had he met her on a footpath she would have walked straight at him.

"What?"

"Is your husband in?"

"You'll be lucky. He was on the piss last night, him and his mates. He won't surface 'til he's hungry."

"But he's in?"

"I said – he won't surface 'til he's hungry or fancies a bit of the other," the woman said with a coarse laugh.

"I need to speak with him."

"He aint here. They came back here from the pub and them pissed off."

"Where?"

The woman, who had not moved from inside her doorway, looked up at the sky and then at Bingham from whose shoulders the rain dripped, but didn't answer.

"He came back from the pub with Matt Pretty?" asked Bingham, hoping to stir a response.

"I said!"

"Where did they piss off to?"

The woman looked at Bingham, unused to his sort swearing. She laughed: his manner had put her at ease. If a man could swear, he must be all right. She'd taken Bingham for a toff; but you can always be wrong about someone.

"Dan's place, I expect. His missus isn't as fussy as me. She doesn't mind clearing up the puke."

"Dan's place is …"

"Hanging Bridge. It's just up the road. He's got a place north of there."

"Thanks."

"Don't mention it. Tell him I don't won't to see him 'til he's sober," she replied, adding, "when he'll be some use to me."

Bingham smiled as he clambered back into his car, hearing her call out before she closed the door.

"Take Birdsgrove Lane! It's off the Swinscoe Hill. Go carefully or you'll miss it. It's on your left, about a mile. Don't go too far! Look for a red roof!"

A good sort, he thought – coarse, but she'd go the extra mile for you. He'd met parents like her and they were always supportive. He wondered how she became mixed up with the friends of Matthew Pretty, but only for a moment.

Back on the B5032, now named the Ashbourne Road, he realised he was driving alongside the River Dove. To the west of the village, he crossed the bridge over the river and headed due north. A sign told him that the Royal Oak Inn was waiting in the village itself, and he wondered how often the men he sought blessed the establishment with their presence.

More lanes, more single tracks, more passing places. On a summer's day it would have been a beautiful drive: the hedges were well kept and overlooked typical English farmland. Ahead, the horizon was decked with trees of all sorts: elms, horse-chestnuts, birches, oaks, almost stripped, now, of their leaves, which lay sodden by the roadside and on the verges. To his left, young sycamores fronted hawthorn hedgerows.

Beyond these, along an even narrower lane, Bingham glimpsed the red roof, which he supposed was that of a barn. So far, he had not come across a police vehicle of any sort and wondered whether even Mark Bawley had arrived, so circuitous had been the route.

He pulled into the space by one of the wooden gates that gave access to the fields, deciding to walk the rest of the way to the farm; he felt the need to arrive unannounced. The Dove wound to his right, only a few hundred yards away as he entered the farmyard. Such a beautiful spot: not one for an atrocity.

Ahead of him, along the lane that now narrowed to little more than a path ran a few chickens that had been grubbing in the verge; further on he heard geese hissing. Never a good sound; they were great guards and he'd been attacked once on an uncle's farm when he was a child.

As he turned into the farmyard, he saw a man, big and one who might 'enjoy a spot of bother'. John Hayes's words came back to Bingham and he paused, wondering what to do next; but the man didn't move. He seemed transfixed, his eyes focussed on something or someone out of sight to Bingham. He moved forward, carefully, although the hissing of the geese would have warned anyone waiting of his arrival.

As the scene opened before him, he saw a man on the ground, his legs spread out, twitching his arms. Bingham was reminded of Raymond Dowdall's description of Janet Bawley after she'd struggled from the copse of birch trees. Several feet from him, stood Mark Bawley, the shotgun in his hand levelled beyond the body, watching the man dying on the concrete of the yard. Another man leaned against a tractor that was parked near the red barn; he, too, was fixed to the spot, unable or unwilling to move. From the doorway of the farmhouse a woman screamed, her hands covering her mouth but failing to muffle the sounds. 'Those who live by the sword, die by the sword', thought Bingham, surprised at his own lack of sympathy for Matthew Pretty because it was he who lay dying.

Only the woman looked up at Bingham, hoping, perhaps, that here was someone who would put right this madness, unaware as she might have been of her own husband's part in the conspiracy that had convicted an innocent boy. Bingham had no doubt that these were the men who had threatened witnesses on Pretty's behalf and pursued John Hayes when he began his investigation.

Bingham walked over to Mark Bawley, unsure what he was going to do but feeling the need to be at one with the man, beside him as a friend.

The dead woman's widower looked up as he approached and almost smiled with what Bingham took to be relief. Mark Bawley could not be described as happy but more pleased as though at last some consolation had come to him. He was a man at ease with himself, one who had finally found solace.

Bingham took the gun from him and held it over his arm in the broken position, and Mark Bawley made a vague gesture in reply, one of gratitude.

As soon as Bingham had the gun, the man by the tractor moved and leaned over the dying man; the other, too, ran forward. The woman came unsteadily towards them, her face asking the obvious question. Both men shook their heads: the man on the yard was beyond the help of any doctor.

All five people held their positions for what seemed ages, no one certain as to what they might do, until a siren was heard on Birdsgrove Lane and, eventually, a police car screamed into the yard. Mark Bawley offered no resistance as he was led to the car; he only looked back over his shoulder and repeated his smile to Bingham, a smile that said as plainly as any words that the memory of his wife's murder had, at last, been assuaged.

EPILOGUE

Bingham was the first person to see Meg Pretty. Lina had offered to accompany him but for reasons he couldn't explain he thought the widow would not appreciate the presence of another woman, and Lina understood.

The bruising around her left eye had now spread down her cheek but, if anything, this only enhanced, however temporarily, the ferocity of her expression. Her eyes still shone with that independent spirit born of nature: one that cannot be acquired through reading. She smiled, when opening the door to Bingham, nodded to a place at the table, offered him a coffee and listened impassively while Bingham related what had happened.

"He got what he deserved," she said, when Bingham had finished.

"How will you cope, running a farm on your own?"

"You're a very practical man, George."

"So, my wife tells me."

"I'll find a farmhand," she replied, giving Bingham a certain look, "There'll be several of Matt's friends who think they may be in with a chance. They'll be round here before I've buried the bugger."

"And you only suspected, as recently as yesterday, that he might be involved in the murder?"

Another look, harder this time.

"I might have suspected earlier."

"From the beginning?"

"Possibly. Are you sure you're not a policeman, George?"

How many of the townsfolk had suspected Raymond Dowdall was likely to be innocent, Bingham wondered; how many had kept quiet, preferring to go on, uninterrupted, with their lives?

"Will the young man be freed now?"

"We've yet to find out whether your husband ..."

"Ex-husband!"

"... can be linked to the murder."

"Isn't it obvious?"

"To you and me and others, no doubt, but have the police enough evidence to convince the courts?"

Bingham's doubts were only lingering ones, but he wasn't going to let Meg Pretty off the hook so easily.

Mehreen Choudhury came to the White Hart a few days later by which time Ben had re-joined his parents, his broken leg encased in a walking boot. "Not that I'll be doing much walking of the kind we'd intended," he'd remarked. Mollie was settled by his side rather than Bingham's, seeming to know, in the way that dogs do, that she owed this young man a debt. John Hayes was also with the Binghams and the four sat drinking coffee when the young police officer arrived, a smile on her face.

When Bingham had brought her a drink, she ran over the details of the false witness statements, the interviews of the three arsonists with both the Suffolk and Staffordshire constabularies and subsequent interviews with Reggie Morton, the owner of the farm where Matthew Pretty had been shot and Walter Higgins.

"We've yet to approach Mr Osman and Mrs Pretty," she continued, "but Chief Inspector Wright feels that we may need to do so ..."

"*May*!", questioned John Hayes, "Osman once boasted that he was the one who finished Janet Bawley off!"

"Chief Inspector Wright always uses cautionary language," replied Mehreen Choudhury, "He meant 'will'. It now seems likely that it was just a boast, but you are right – he *may* know something of interest. The chief inspector is keen to clear this matter up, and so do not doubt his sincerity. He has already invited PC Charlton to the station ..."

"*Invited*!" said John Hayes.

"It was a productive meeting ... May I continue?"

"Sorry," said the newspaperman, and slumped back into his seat.

"You will remember that our original informant was a police officer, a young constable at the time of the murder. It was he who brought the false witness statements to our attention. He was, naturally, concerned about losing his pension rights if he came forward, as well as breaching the Official Secrets Act. Chief Inspector Wright persuaded him to approach a London solicitor to discuss these issues and he received the reassurance he needed to make a statement directly to the Criminal Cases Review Commission."

"That is wonderful news, PC Choudhury," said John Hayes.

"It is only the first step," she replied, "but it will open up the need to conduct further interviews with the parties concerned."

"It will be a marathon legal struggle," said John Hayes, "Raymond's defence lawyers will have a fight on their hands when they attempt to prepare another appeal."

"Softly, softly," replied Mehreen Choudhury.

Bingham couldn't help but think that there were many monkeys who would be reluctant to be caught.

It was a week later, when the Binghams were home enjoying another coffee time – on this occasion in their kitchen, their four dogs having overcome the initial excitement settled peacefully on the tiled floor – that a letter arrived from John Hayes.

Dear Lina, George and Ben,

I trust life is treating you well. It goes on up here much as usual. I was not expecting speedy action from the constabulary and I have not been disappointed. But to be fair, there are signs that things are moving in the right direction. I have had an altercation with Bill Charlton that suggests he is rattled.

As you know, he and I have never been the best of friends and he roused my dander again this last week when I heard he had been sounding off in one of his usual haunts – the Golden Lion at Denstone. According to our Mr Charlton, he sent me off with a flea in my ear when I went around to his house. Since I distinctly remember him being very hot under the collar with evasion written in every line of his face when I left, I found that particularly annoying.

I thought I would confront him and knew he was involved with the local darts team, and so I made a few enquiries (you cannot keep an old newspaper man down!) and discovered they were playing against an Ellastone team. I decided to go along and have a word. I found him propping up the bar with some of his mates – big lads who would not say no to a spot of bother. I was fairly angry and so I beckoned him over. He looked smug but I could see it was all a pose and decided to go for him.

I told him he was a disgrace to his uniform, a 'bent penny' (I picked that one up from George Dixon many years ago: remember Dixon of Dock Green, George?) and that if he had done his job honourably, as any decent copper would, his mate, Matthew Penny, would have been doing time (and probably out on parole by now!) instead of lying dead in a farmyard.

He didn't like that I can tell you! He turned purple with rage. His mates began to mutter, there were some nasty looks and there was talk of sorting me out, but the wind has been taken from their sails and they are floundering.

I decided to go one step further and challenged Charlton to be man enough to tell the truth of his own free will before it was rung out of him in court. He did a bit of mumbling about the Official Secrets Act, but his hard-man image had crumbled in front of his mates, and that was enough for me.

I hope you are all well and look forward to seeing you in Upton as soon as we get some hopeful news. Thanks for all your help with Raymond's appeal. It's been a long haul for me, but thanks to you we are now seeing the light at the end of the tunnel.

Your good friend,
John Hayes

"He's a brave man," said Bingham, looking across the table at his wife who had sat motionless, not to say spellbound, while Bingham read out the journalist's letter, "He pursued these villains, alone, hampered by officialdom and threatened with being murdered himself. He worked tirelessly over so many years, while still holding down his own job, collecting evidence that was rejected or ignored, trying to illicit information from people reluctant to talk. I cannot but admire the man. He deserves a knighthood."

*

A further year passed before Raymond Dowdall gained his freedom, a year spent gathering and collating evidence indisputable enough to convince the Court of Appeal that a miscarriage of justice had occurred; for it is a tenet of British justice that the Law is never wrong. There was no apology for the years he had spent, wrongfully, in prison and not a hint of sympathy from the appeal court judges, nor was he ever declared innocent despite his conviction being squashed.

Mark Bawley pleaded guilty and was convicted of the murder of Matthew Pretty and sentenced to fourteen years in prison. (The coincidental length of the sentence was not lost of those who remembered Raymond's time in prison.) On appeal, his defence argued that provocation had brought about a 'loss of control' (a term that has almost replaced the concept of a 'crime of passion') and the sentence was reduced to seven years. The widower showed no remorse but acknowledged his guilt and was released on parole after serving four years of his sentence. He returned to the house he had shared with his wife, Janet, and set himself up privately as a surveyor.

Reggie Morton and Walter Higgins were convicted of being accessories to the original crime; their defence argued that they were accessories *after* the fact. Although doubt remained as to whether this was the case with the hotelier, it was considered indisputable with regard to Walter Higgins. Both men were sentenced to two years in prison; both were released from this sentence after a year.

On the charge of arson, the man who had refused to give his name was sentenced to five years year in prison, as was Walter Higgins, but the young man, Martin Newham, was given a community service order, it being argued by his defence team that a custodial sentence was likely to do more harm than good and that several members of his local community, including John Hayes, as well as the man whose house he threatened, George Bingham, had spoken in his defence.

Phil Bassett was charged with Grievous Bodily Harm, a crime that carries a maximum custodial sentence of five years. He was persuaded to opt to be tried in a magistrate's court, where the sentence was reduced to six months. Since it was considered that there had been 'contributory, aggravating factors' (he was protecting his friend's house from arsonists), his sentence was suspended for two years. Phil remained proud of what he had done but was persuaded to refrain from expressing this in court.

Raymond Dowdall, on his release, showed no bitterness, no words of recrimination passed his lips and he praised the efforts of 'those officers of the Staffordshire police force who have been active in clearing my name'. He is currently working on a book, alongside his work with Mr Roberts at the estate agency, about the historical architecture of the buildings of Upton-on-Churnet.

Autumn 2019

AUTHOR'S NOTE AND ACKNOWLEDGEMENTS

Although this story is a fiction, its key events and descriptions are based on actual incidents and the experiences of people involved in similar situations and circumstances. The young man at the centre of Bingham's search was suggested by someone my wife knows; the search for truth in his case was conducted by a newspaperman. Anyone wishing to delve deeper into the real world from which this novel is drawn should read:

Town Without Pity by Don Hale OBE
Century, Random House 2002

All the characters in this book are fictitious and any resemblance to persons, living or dead, is purely coincidental.